EVIL GENIUS

ALSO BY CLAIRE OSHETSKY

Chouette

Poor Deer

The Book of Dog by Lark Benobi

EVIL GENIUS

A NOVEL

CLAIRE OSHETSKY

ecco
An Imprint of HarperCollins*Publishers*

 For information, address HarperCollins Publishers, 195 Broadway, New York, NY 10007. In Europe, HarperCollins Publishers, Macken House, 39/40 Mayor Street Upper, Dublin 1, D01 C9W8, Ireland.

HarperCollins books may be purchased for educational, business, or sales promotional use. For information, please email the Special Markets Department at SPsales@harpercollins.com.

hc.com

FIRST EDITION

Designed by Alison Bloomer
Background Image © Oleksandr Yashchuk / Shutterstock

Library of Congress Cataloging-in-Publication Data
Names: Oshetsky, Claire author
Title: Evil genius: a novel / Claire Oshetsky.
Description: First edition. | New York, NY: Ecco, 2026.
Identifiers: LCCN 2025014120 (print) | LCCN 2025014121 (ebook) | ISBN 9780063466487 hardcover | ISBN 9780063466500 trade paperback | ISBN 9780063466494 ebook
Subjects: LCGFT: Fiction | Noir fiction | Novels
Classification: LCC PS3615.S39 E95 2026 (print) | LCC PS3615.S39 (ebook) | DDC 813/.6—dc23/eng/20250602
LC record available at https://lccn.loc.gov/2025014120
LC ebook record available at https://lccn.loc.gov/2025014121

26 27 28 29 30 LBC 6 5 4 3 2

FOR MY SISTERS

Anne Margaret Oshetsky

Ellen Irene Zensen

I think about you every day.

Afoot and light-hearted I take to the open road,
Healthy, free, the world before me,
The long brown path before me leading wherever I choose.

Walt Whitman

CONTENTS

ONE

THE CLIFFHANGER

I didn't mourn for Vivienne Bianco. I didn't know her. I knew how she died, though, because Randall Smiley told me the whole terrible story. I couldn't get Randall's story out of my head. I was never again going to let myself forget how each breath was bringing me closer to my final breath. How would I live differently? For sure I didn't want to live the same life I'd been living. I craved revolutionary changes in my life. Violent changes, even. I felt like I was exercising a new muscle in my body. My body began to conform to my new way of thinking. Each day my body grew more loose-limbed and intuitive. It grew more sensitive to things. Trivial things at first, like the way my clothes felt against my skin as I walked along. Then larger things, too, and larger-than-large things—profound things, even—like the boundless sky at dusk when work was done. A slant-sun would be making its way toward the horizon, and the east-west roads would be orange and glowing. The traffic would begin to shift feverishly in all directions, and my body would tremble on the breezes—and away I would fly, like a muscular swan. Or so it seemed to me.

The year was 1974. I was nineteen years old. Newspapers kept running a photograph of an internationally famous heiress toting a machine gun while wearing a saucy beret. One day on my lunch break I bought a saucy beret for myself, at a hat store on Market Street. There were hat stores in those days. Berets were fashionable among radicals and the very old. The world was a noisy, crowded place in that era. You couldn't walk down a simple street without your head intersecting with a radio wave or a casual sidewalk conversation.

I worked for the phone company that year, in the Resident Billing Office, on the third floor of a six-floor building on Fourth Street in San Francisco. Randall Smiley worked on the same floor as I did, but six rows over. Our job was to make people pay their phone bills. The job was uniquely powerful because in those days the telephone was all there was. No world wide web. No texting. No picturephones, either, although they'd been promised to us ever since the New York World's Fair in 1964. If you wanted to speak to somebody who wasn't within shouting distance then you talked through a box, attached with a wire to a wall. Back then the phone was so important that we who worked in the Resident Billing Office were like harsh cold gods. If you didn't pay on time, or if we didn't like your tone, or if you disrespected us, then we could disconnect your phone as fast as a fingersnap and you'd be dead to the world. We called it *ripping your lips*. We'd say: "Don't get testy with me, Mister Customer! If you don't pay up by Friday, I'm going to rip your lips!"

But our job was uniquely powerless, too, because for eight hours a day we were tethered to a short cord attached to a headset. We were forbidden to leave our workstations unless we got permission. To get permission we needed to hold up a little paddle. Then we needed to wait until the floor supervisor noticed the paddle and excused us. The floor supervisors were all men who didn't understand about menstruation. All day long they sat up on a dais at the front of the room and surveyed us like petty dictators, with their arms crossed. On any given day the floor supervisor might decide to flex his petty-dictator muscles and pretend not to see our paddle and leave us bleeding or peeing in our pants or otherwise embarrassing ourselves.

The queue of customers calling in to explain why they hadn't paid their phone bills never ended. Every three minutes a different voice made its way into our ears. Three minutes was all the time we were supposed to take on each call. The voice might be drunk, or belligerent, or hostile, or afraid of the dark. The voice might be suicidal. The voice might be full of desperation. By the end of each day an everlasting chorus of voices filled our heads. Berating us. Pleading with us. Threatening us. We weren't supposed to hang up. The best we could do if a customer was drunk or obscene or abusive was to switch the call over to a floor supervisor. Once a floor supervisor took over the call then those randy, rowdy voices would settle down, usually. They'd respond to a floor supervisor's voice differently. They'd be gentle and polite and reasonable. When the call was done, the floor supervisor would come over to my station and say, "What's the matter with you, Celia? That man was a perfect gentleman. You must have done something to rouse him!"

Our work life was so regimented that we needed to find drama elsewhere, in our off-hours.

Here is the drama Randall Smiley found. He was carrying on with Vivienne Bianco.

Vivienne worked at the phone company, too, but she was four steps up the corporate ladder from Randall and me. Sometimes she wore a yellow suit to work. Sometimes a navy one. No matter what the color of her suit, her blouse was always tastefully cream-colored. She had the typical rigid stern posture that all career women of that era adopted. Solid shoes. Big bows. Beyond sharing an elevator with her now and then—I worked on the third floor, and she, the sixth—I didn't know Vivienne Bianco. None of us knew her. She was literally on another level from us Resident Billing workers, and for the life of us we couldn't understand why she'd chosen Randall Smiley, of all people, to be her love nest companion, because Randall was shaped like a beach ball with legs sticking out below and his hair was unwashed. Randall had lovely strong hands, though, and he spoke in a manly and commanding voice. His was the kind of voice you could imagine coming out of the mouths of four-star generals or sea captains. And maybe Randall had other fine qualities, too, not to be perceived in the course of daily polite society, and maybe he felt like a safe bet to her, because for sure she'd never run across him accidentally at one of her fancy corporate soirees or at a neighborhood bridge party. She and Randall moved in different circles. All these speculations kept us billing operators busy gossiping about Vivienne and Randall on our breaks, and we could never agree on what had brought those lovers together, because the ways of love are meandering and mysterious.

The two of them used to go to her place in Pacific Heights.

One day her husband came home at an inopportune time.

"Get under the bed, get under the bed!" Vivienne ugly-whispered, and Randall had done exactly that, squeezing himself under the bed—but in their panic the two lovers forgot to attend to the used condom on the floor. Talk about incriminating evidence. The rest of us could only imagine Randall's sickening embarrassment at needing to testify at the trial.

But wait. I'm telling it all wrong. It's because of the paddle situation.

Let me try again.

Because of the paddle situation it was nearly impossible to get the floor supervisors to excuse me at the same time that Randall took his break. That's why, for the last four days—ever since Vivienne had met her grisly end, that is—I'd only heard the story in bits and dribs of secondhand gossip. Everyone was frantically trying to hold up their paddles at the same time Randall held up his paddle for his break. All of us wanted to hear the story from Randall's own lips. But only four of us were allowed to unplug from the call queue at any one time. Otherwise the queue would spill into the day after next. Customers would be hanging on the line for so long that they'd wander away from their telephones or hang up and call again, which created an awful mess by the end of the day.

Despite these obstacles, eventually I found myself sitting in the designated break room for smokers, with Randall Smiley sitting across from me, telling his tale to us eager listeners. There were people from every floor crammed in. People had ignored the break rooms on their own floors and had come to the third floor on the off chance that their break would coincide with Randall's. There we were, we lucky few, huddled around a sticky square table with nothing on it but overflowing ashtrays. The story Randall told us that day begins with two lovers dreamily dozing in Vivienne's big bed in Pacific Heights. It's love. It's really love. Randall kept telling us eager listeners it was really love.

Suddenly Vivienne hears a key rattling in the lock on the

front door downstairs and she ugly-whispers, "Dear Lord, it's Gene! Hide, Randall, hide!" And Randall, being a phone company man with no imagination, dives under the bed. He hears heavy shoes on the stairs. The sound is coming closer, step by step—imagine Randall telling this part of the story like the campfire story kids used to tell each other, at summer camp: *Mary, I'm on the first step; Mary, I'm on the second step*—and his heart won't stop its fearful clatter.

That's when Randall sees the used condom over there, on the floor, right at Randall's eye level, and he wants to say: "Get the condom, Vivienne!"—but his courage fails him, and then it's too late, and so he swallows his warning and bites one knuckle. If only there had been more time. If only.

As for Vivienne, she, too, is a creature of the phone company, and she has unimaginatively decided to play sick-in-bed, but it's no good, because her hair is messy in an undeniably sexy way, and not in a sickbed sort of way. True, she is looking flushed but it's by no means the flush of a sick woman. It's an unmistakable postcoital flush, because Randall has put the bloom back in Vivienne's cheeks. Oh yes, my dears. That poor woman should have gone straight to the bathroom and locked the door behind her and claimed some kind of bowel complaint had kept her home from work. I was thinking that's what I would have done in those circumstances. All of us were thinking about what we would have done in those circumstances. Where we would have hidden. How we would have explained. How we would have escaped the coming confrontation. Suddenly Randall sees the husband's boots in the doorway. They're heavy boots. The kind that can break ribs, crack skulls. The husband's name is Gene Bianco and he is president of a company that sells tractors and other farm equipment. He is supposed to be at a tractor convention in Des Moines this week but here he is in the flesh. Randall holds his breath. He didn't tell us the part about holding his breath. Those of us listening to his story intuited it. We were holding our own breath in sympathy.

What the hell, Vivienne! the husband yells.

He's enraged even before he sees the incriminating jism-filled evidence on the floor. He isn't buying his wife's sick-day excuse. Then he does see the incriminating evidence. From under the bed, Randall watches a hairy-knuckled hand reaching down for that evidence, and then the husband shouts the same thing all over again, but louder:

What the hell, Vivienne?—

And then? The roar of a gun.

Here in the designated break room for smokers, Randall paused.

"Gawd, Randall," drawled a woman from the second floor.

I knew this woman a little. Her name was Meena, and she had snuck up from the second floor to the third floor and I didn't blame her because on her floor nothing interesting ever happened. A year ago someone on her floor delivered unexpected triplets. That was it for the second floor in the drama department.

Randall coughed and went on with his story.

All is still. All is dreadfully, dreadfully still.

Then the stillness is broken by the sound of the husband's voice, only now the husband's voice sounds like the voice of a child.

Viv? the husband whispers.

He's too stunned by his own crime of passion to wonder where the man who filled the incriminating condom with his anemic spurts might be. The thought of this other man has been wiped from the husband's mind by the sight of his wife, now a corpse.

By this time in the story the smoke in our smokers' break room was thick and our break time had come to an end but we all lit a second one. We were in no hurry to go back. We smoked our second cigarette and went on to our third. We should have been back at our workstations six minutes ago. To be honest discipline had been lax on the entire floor recently. Ever since Vivienne's fate was sealed, the entire building had been infected by a chaotic flouting of the rules. But anyway. Let us return to Randall, under the bed, cheek to cheek with Vivienne's silk rug. The crazed husband's boots are pointed right at him. The husband is so quiet and still that Randall can hear the aftershock of the gunshot ringing in his ears. He's sure the husband is about to look under the bed and see him and he'd shoot Randall straight between the eyes with the bullet in the next chamber.

Viv? the husband says.

He says his wife's name like it's the sweetest declaration of love.

Is that you, Vivienne? he says.

And when Vivienne still doesn't answer, the husband says: *Come on, Vivienne! Don't mess with me!*

And when Vivienne has nothing to say about that, either, the husband gives up trying to get a rise out of her and flings himself down on the bed next to his wife's body—or maybe, on top of it; Randall, under the bed, and with a limited view of the scene above, really can't say for sure—and sobs. The husband is a big man. The mattress pushes down on Randall and he can barely breathe. He can tell from the stillness of Vivienne's hand, flopped over, that she's a goner. Blood is dripping from her fingertips. Blood is hanging in the air in microscopic droplets and everything is tinged with a pinkish yellow haze and Randall can feel a sneeze coming on.

"Gawd, Randall," drawled the woman from downstairs again. Meena.

That's when our floor supervisor burst in and fresh smokeless air poured in after him—"What are you people doing in here? The phones are ringing *off the hook*!"—and what could we do? We stood up and looked at each other with stupefied faces as if we'd all somehow forgotten the time, and we went back to work.

I scuttled to my station and plugged in.

So did Randall Smiley, six rows over.

"This is Celia, how can I help you?" I said into my headset.

Sometimes I told the Resident Billing customers my name was Celia. Sometimes I said I was Operator 737. Both were correct. Both followed the company rules. I never said, "This is Celia Dent, how can I help you?" because the company rule was never to divulge our full names.

The customer on the other end of the line told me her name was Mrs. Robert Brisket. She emphasized the "Missus." She sounded exasperated. She told me she'd just opened the phone bill, only to discover that her son was addicted to phone porno. When I looked up Mrs. Brisket's bill in our system, I whistled. Every ninety seconds for the last eighteen days, between midnight and four a.m., there was a new dollar-fifty charge on the bill.

"I can't possibly pay this bill," Mrs. Brisket said. "I didn't know. What do I do?"

People were calling in all the time to tell me their troubles and excuses for why their phone bill couldn't be paid on time. They'd tell me they didn't know it was a dollar a minute to speak to their sister in Ottawa. Or they didn't know when they accepted the charges for a phone call from their boyfriends in San Quentin that it meant they needed to pay for those charges. Or they didn't know their son was dialing up phone porno recordings in the middle of the night. It was easy to get swayed by their sob stories, and to forget that my primary purpose was to protect the company. We're supposed to be kind, but we're also supposed to collect. While Mrs. Brisket was pleading with me in my left ear, I could hear the rattle of a gurgly voice in my right ear, telling me, *You've got to rip this woman's lips, as surely as your life depends on it.* Mrs. Brisket's bill was six thousand four hundred and eighty dollars. I ripped her lips. Later I would think, oh, gosh, maybe I shouldn't have listened to that gurgly voice in my right ear. Maybe I should have been kinder to poor Mrs. Brisket. I could have tried to work out a payment schedule for her. We're allowed to do that in special circumstances, with a floor supervisor's okay. But I was distracted from my compassionate side by the fate of Vivienne Bianco. I was lost in a hazy fog of wonderment about the violent ways lovers settle their differences. The story of Vivienne Bianco's grisly end had put me in a mood, half disapproving and half aroused, and I ripped people's lips left and right all afternoon.

It was close to quitting time when one of the floor supervisors walked over to Randall Smiley's desk along with two security guards. Those guards escorted Randall Smiley away, to parts unknown. Word flurried through the rows and desks of my fellow billing workers that Randall was about to get the boot. If the rumor was true, and if Randall really was about to get the boot, then I'd never hear how he got out of his sticky pickle. I'd never know how the story ended. I'd be stuck forever at the cliffhanger, with poor Randall Smiley hiding there, under the bed, a mattress-width away from a jealous, raging, uncontrollably sobbing husband with a gun in his hand.

TWO

A DROP OF WINE

It's a strange but true fact that a typical person living in these modern times will cross paths with thirty-six actual, in-the-flesh murderers during their lifetime, along with seventy-seven people who are destined to be murdered. Real-life murderers pass us by in the streets with nary a whisper or a sign. Real-life victims pass us by at about twice the rate as the murderers do. Most of the time the murderer is a man, but not always. There are women capable of killing. There are layers upon layers of love-and-death happenings going on every second in this world while we walk on blithely. Most of the time these violent crimes happen behind closed doors, in a domestic situation that from the outside looks reasonably content, but experience proves you can never know for sure what's happening or about to happen right next door, or closer, in your very own home. That's what I always say.

So maybe it's not so surprising that Vivienne Bianco wasn't the first person I'd met whose life-journey led them to a blood-soaked final destination. When I was a girl I heard about a woman in the next town over who'd murdered her husband. My mother knew the woman, but not so well. This woman loved to sew, and so did my mother, and sometimes the two of them would cross paths in their favorite fabric store, where they would make small talk about sewing patterns, or buttons, and whether they preferred a French knot to a colonial knot, but their friendship never went any further. I was at an age where I liked to crawl between the big bolts of fabric in the store, to hide there. My mother would search the store, calling my name—*Celia! Celia!*—and sometimes the murderous woman would join in the search. Often it was she who found me first. I fondly remember the look of that woman's jolly red round face as she bent down and spied me in my hiding place. I remember her dear smile. "Come on out of there, you little monkey!" she'd whisper, and the way she spoke to me made me feel as if the two of us had a special conspiratorial relationship.

Or sometimes, instead of hiding myself away behind the big bolts of fabric, I would sidle up secretly to the measuring table, and when no one was looking I'd steal the big scissors from the tabletop. I'd walk away with those scissors tucked inside the folds of my skirt. I was small and stealthy and girlish in those days. I could walk along as if invisible. No one suspected me of malice or deception, because of my sweet ways. I would make my invisible way through the rows and rows of fabric bolts with those big scissors hidden in my skirt. A feeling would come over me and I would compulsively make sharp cuts, deep into the fabric. No one ever knew I was the one who had defiled the cloth. I loved to watch the cloth divide in two between the scissors-blades. I loved the nearly-not-a-sound sound those sharp scissors made, so close to the sound of a soft voice whispering. Sometimes I'd spare them—those big fabric bolts—and walk on without defiling them. I'd slap them as I passed by, though, as a warning that next time I would not go so easy on them. Those bolts of fabric felt like thick legs to me, or like headless torsos. They had a warmth to them. They felt like living things.

The point is my mother and this woman weren't really friends. They were fabric-store friends. Nonetheless, when my mother heard the news about what had happened between that woman and her husband, she felt a big feeling well up inside. It wasn't shock or fear. She hadn't known the woman well enough for shock or fear. In fact, I think the news exhilarated her. Or maybe she felt as if she'd personally dodged a bullet. For weeks my mother chatted energetically on the telephone with her friends about her narrow escape. The conversations were lively and speculative.

"We were very, very close," my mother would say into the phone.

She would leave the impression that she might well have been visiting the woman in her home on the fateful day. There they were, two friendly seamstresses, sitting contentedly in the kitchen together, sipping tea and chatting away about the pleasures of sewing a hem by hand, when a door opens, and the husband comes sauntering in without the barest idea he is about to die—and the wife rushes forward! Knife raised! She does the deed!

"Stabbed him to *death*," my mother would whisper into the telephone.

And then she'd remember she was a mother and that walls had ears and would look around frantically to make sure I wasn't eavesdropping on her sordid tale. But of course I was eavesdropping, because her tale was about love and death, life's two greatest mysteries. When she spied me there in the corner hanging onto her every word, she would scold me and tell me to scoot and go play in my room.

You will probably not be so surprised to learn that the idea of stabbing somebody to *death* or alternatively being stabbed to *death* myself soon took hold of my child-mind. It was all I could think about. I owned three Barbie dolls back then. I didn't take good care of them. My mother was always sewing my Barbie dolls darling little outfits to match my own, but the tiny buttons and snaps were too delicate for my blunt child-fingers, and I would leave those dolls naked and thrown on the floor. I disliked their unmoving faces. I'd given them all haircuts, but the results were disappointing because I could see the tiny circular holes in their scalps where the fake hair had been threaded through, and the holes disturbed me.

One day I lined up those dolls on the floor of my bedroom and stabbed them experimentally with my mother's nail file. Their legs and arms and breasts were hard plastic and could easily withstand my childish stabs. The heads were another matter. They were hollow and rubbery. The nail file went right through those flabby faces, and I felt something close to a sexual thrill. At that age, I had no idea what a sexual thrill felt like. But when I think back on the memory, now that I have experienced ever so many of life's erotic pleasures, "sexual thrill" is a close approximation of the way I remember feeling as a girl when I stabbed those dolls in the eye.

Later in life I would feel slightly ashamed of myself. To make up for what I had done to those poor rubbery faces, I began to collect Barbie dolls in earnest. I took loving care of them. I never took those dolls out of their boxes. My mother encouraged my interest. She cleared out the pantry. Together we put up shelves and painted them pink. Over the years, my collection grew.

Every birthday and every Christmas and every time I got an A on my report card, my mother gifted me a new doll for my collection. But it was maybe too late to reform me. The match had been lit. Danger and sex and passion and violence and tragic endings were all knotted up inside of me by then, long before I knew what any of those words really meant.

After a certain *event* occurred when I was eleven, and which I will maybe tell you about some other time, my mother was constantly looking at me askance.

"You're getting wilder every day," she liked to say. "You're going to turn out exactly like your father."

I began to wonder about this father of mine and how he had turned out. He'd been out of the picture since before I could remember, and that absence, that void in my past, made him an object of mythic fascination in my mind even before my mother began to constantly remind me that my father had existed and had helped give rise to me. Who was this man she called "your father"? The only thing my mother would ever say about him was that he'd been a bounder. But what was it about me, in particular, that reminded my mother of my father, the bounder? Was he alive or dead? What the heck was a bounder? My mother wouldn't say. Whenever I asked her about my father, she told me to mind my own business.

Maybe there was evidence of a father figure somewhere in the house, stuffed behind a drawer or in the attic or in one of my mother's many sewing baskets. I began to look for clues whenever my mother was out. I was sixteen when I found a black-and-white photograph of a man I didn't know. I found it in a box full of stale yellow letters. He was biting an unlit cigarette between his teeth and squinting. As soon as he'd seen me looking back at him, he'd instantly begun to beguile me with his sorry tale.

"You've found me out, kid, and what your mother told you about me is true—I *am* a bounder!" he said. I felt an immediate kinship with this man's reckless attitude toward life and its obligations. I respected the way he cocked his head to one side. On the back of the photograph, in my mother's rounded handwriting, was one word. The word was: *Dirk*. It intrigued me no end to imagine that my father had been named at birth for a stabbing blade once favored by Highland assassins.

And so I kept that photograph. I didn't tuck it back into the box of yellow faded letters. Instead, I put it away, in a special place known only to me, where I'd begun to collect all the threads and clues and hidden mysteries of life. I was certain one day I would collect enough clues to explain all I needed to know about weighty metaphysical matters. I'd already collected three Barbie doll heads, still scarred from my childhood days, plus a pair of sewing scissors, plus an old nail file that had once belonged to my mother—and to this burgeoning collection of life-clues, I added a photo of a man named Dirk, who might have been a bounder, and also, my dad.

Not so many days after I'd stashed away the photo of my maybe-father in my secret place, my mother began to see things. Shadows, mostly, where they didn't belong. Over the days and weeks to come, she grew ever more fearful of her body being taken over by these shadows. She sealed the windows shut in every room. She never went out of the house if she could help it. For hours on end she sat in her favorite armchair, and knitted, and wove, and tatted tiny small hexagonal hexes with her jittery sick hands. She nailed these small symbols above every doorway and window of the house. "To keep the chaos out," she told me.

My mother had been born in the old country, coming to these shores only at the age of nine, and she never rejected the superstitious pagan beliefs that had served her ancestors so well and had been passed on by countless generations of simple agrarian folk. Some of my mother's hexes had symmetric repeating patterns sewn into them. Some depicted mythic beasts. Some were strange stick figures, with triangles for heads. I thought my mother was cracked. Her mind was confused by then. Her skin was gray. Her eyes were glazed. Her brain was full of holes. Her thinking grew conspiratorial. She was convinced I was trying to poison her. "Keep away, keep away!" she would shout, and then her eyes would grow wide and she'd begin to sob, and she would ask me to forgive her. Her ailments grew more fearsome each day. Whenever she needed to stay overnight at the hospital, she would wake in the night, screaming: "The shadows, the shadows!" until the nurses came and sedated her. I was nearly eighteen when a mysterious wasting disease finally took her from me. After she passed, I left her hexes up over the windows and doors. They had become part of the home decor. I didn't think about it until my Drew moved in. Drew said those scraps of fabric my mother had nailed up were no more than deranged remnants of a past best forgotten. He set to work taking them down.

I had mixed feelings about Drew's plan to purge my mother's house of her hexes, but I admired his can-do attitude. I felt ready to put my mother's grotesque superstitions to rest. As soon as Drew prized the first nail out of the wall with his clever claw hammer, though, I felt a sudden change in the miasmatic pressure inside the house, and I knew for a fact that chaos was a living thing, and I had just welcomed it in.

"Did you feel that?" I said.

"Feel what?" he said.

Drew's reply was a disappointment. It indicated a certain coarseness in his sense of proprioception, to my mind. The abrupt change in the house had felt as obvious to me as a sudden drop in barometric pressure before the coming storm. Already I could hear the wind. Batting at the window sashes. Scuttling past my ears.

Randall Smiley got the boot so close to quitting time that there was no way for us to learn exactly why. We needed to rely on rumors alone. That was the way of the phone company. They kept us workers in the dark for as long as possible, thinking maybe we would forget whatever it was we had questions about, and usually they were right. The prevailing rumor in Randall Smiley's case was that he'd been canned for spending too many minutes of the day in the designated break room for smokers, regaling his eager audience with his tale of love and death. He was gone so fast that we didn't have the chance to ask him if that was the reason.

As I rode the train home that night, past the glass towers and beyond the bay and on into the belly of Redwood City—the town where I'd been born and raised, and where I currently lived with my Drew—my mind was abuzz with back-and-forth conversations with myself about how Randall Smiley's story might have ended. How did Randall free himself from his precarious situation under Vivienne Bianco's big bed? Did he rely on the element of surprise, clambering out from under there and running for his life so fast that the cuckolded murdering husband never had time to shoot? Did he wait, praying under there for a miracle, until the husband made his getaway in his rust-colored pickup truck, giving Randall the chance to crawl out from under that literal deathbed—never daring to look his former lover in the eye—as he skulked away shamefully from his love-tryst gone awry? Did he leap up in a manly manner and wrestle the gun away from the shocked cuckolded murderer's hands and hold him at gunpoint until the police arrived at the scene? Did he hold Gene Bianco in his arms while the repentant, grieving murderer, stunned by his own act of violence, sobbed into his former rival's bare and sweaty shoulder, and found solace there? I didn't know the answer. I would probably never know. I felt intensely irritable about the way Randall got the boot before telling me how he got away from Gene Bianco. It's not that I was excited to imagine a dead woman who had once been my boss's boss's boss's boss lying naked and bleeding on a sateen-sheeted bed with half her head blown away and with her crazed husband lying next to her and her terrified lover hiding underneath. I was shocked and sad about Vivienne's fate. Of course, that. I hated the way women always got the unfortunate end of the stick. On the other hand, I didn't know Vivienne Bianco. I'd shared an elevator with her now and then and that was it.

Just as the train pulled out of the San Carlos station, one station north of where I got off every night, a sudden notion came into my head that maybe Vivienne Bianco's last living moments—the passion, the terror—had so much feeling in them that she'd used up her quota of both passion and terror for an entire lifetime. And then, she died of course. This notion I'd come up with to explain her final moments to myself—moments so full of feeling that her life had come to a natural stopping point, like fireworks—the way they pop off in the night in a glorious display, only to die, leaving nothing but the smell of gunpowder and some ghostly sifting clouds of ash behind—felt romantic and true. Maybe Vivienne had been a profligate waster of her life quota of passion and terror. Maybe she'd used up all the feeling she was meant to feel in this lifetime in those last erotic terror-moments, and then she'd been, you know, *snuffed out*, in a brief candle sort of way. I could suppose it. I liked the idea. It didn't sound like such an awful way to go compared with a lifetime of lonely bored hours working as a billing operator, tethered to a workstation, forced to listen to the dull average woes of all the people in this world, only to return home every night to a less-than-ideal domestic situation. Such was my life. I'm sorry. That's awful of me. I knew it was awful of me. I should have felt compassion for the poor dead Vivienne Bianco but instead of compassion I was feeling something close to sexual frustration. The train cackled along the tracks and then it seemed to sing out in a new and catchy rhythm of a song: *Love and death. Love and death. Love and death.* I almost missed my stop.

I stepped off the train just in time and the doors slid shut. By then I'd filled my head with so many fresh supposings about *love and death* that the train station looked completely unfamiliar. I couldn't remember where I'd parked my mother's Oldsmobile that morning. It took twenty minutes to find it in the lot. When I did find it, I discovered that the front window on the driver's side was smashed in. Bits of glass littered the driver's seat. It wasn't the first time the car had been broken into, but this time it felt like a greater violation, because the ravagers had found my bag of dirty laundry in the back seat. They had gleefully strewn my intimate personal items all over the place. Those miscreants had even tied a pair of my dirty panties onto my radio antenna. There my panties flew, like a sorry pennant. When I took those panties down from the antenna they felt sticky and wet in my hands. It was an ugly end to a confusing day, and my thoughts were galloping. I picked up all the dirty clothes and threw them into the trunk. I used an old towel to sweep away the broken glass from the driver's seat and got in.

Now that I was in the car, moving forward, my mood became upbeat and optimistic. It occurred to me I could go anywhere. I was literally in the driver's seat. I could drive in any direction I pleased. To Mexico, or Canada, or all the way to New York City, or straight into the Pacific Ocean if I wanted. I had never once sat behind the wheel of my mother's Oldsmobile and said to myself, "Okay, Celia, where to?"—and the idea was so startling that I almost went ahead and drove off in an entirely unlikely direction where no one would ever find me again, and if I'd acted on my impulse then this story would have turned out differently, but at the last minute I was cowed by my own instincts, and afraid of what I might be capable of out there on my own, and so I drove straight home, where I knew my Drew would be waiting for me.

My Drew was a man with steady hands and a calm demeanor. He worked at the hospital as a scrub tech, a profession in which steady hands and a calm demeanor are a boon. Drew and I met after my mother got sick. My mother died in peace because she knew there would always be a Drew in my life to take care of me. Drew was a man full of righteous conviction. Maybe that's what I loved most about him—the way he took principled stands on matters of right and wrong. It was a lonely time in my life when we met. I was seventeen and my mother was dying. Here is this guy, dressed in scrubs, sitting alone in the TV room at the hospital watching *The Young and the Restless*, and noticing my distress, and asking me if I'm all right. We talk. He tells me how sorry he is to hear about my mother's struggles. His body is lithe and coiled. His legs are shorter than his torso. There is an easy grace in his movements. He moves like a river otter. I have heard that suggestible people can make up all kinds of things about somebody based on their looks. I've also heard that eyes are windows to the soul. What they don't tell you is that sometimes eyes are shuttered windows, and what's behind them is hidden away. I thought Drew's eyes were deep and wise. I believed in those eyes. Three weeks after we met, Drew kissed me. He'd taken his time. His tongue felt like a hot knife in my throat. He was my first lover, technically speaking. It was easy for me to fall in love with a man like Drew.

When I got home Drew was already in the kitchen, contemplatively shaping a slab of ground meat into well-rounded patties. Ground meat shaped into well-rounded patties was Drew's specialty.

"Hi, honey," I said.

"How was your day?" Drew asked me amiably.

I began to tell Drew all about the death of Vivienne Bianco. I couldn't help myself. I felt the need to speak jubilantly about passion, and mortality, and all I had learned about both, because I wanted Drew to understand me, and because we were committed partners. I told him about Gene Bianco's big boots in the doorway. I carried on merrily with my true-crime story to the end. I thought the expression on my husband's face was amazement, but I was wrong.

"That's disgusting," Drew said, after I'd come to the part where the husband, Gene Bianco, throws himself down upon that literal deathbed. "You're disgusting, Celia. I don't understand you at all. A woman died. And you sound turned on by it. That's disgusting. You're disgusting. I swear, sometimes you scare me half to death. There is something wrong with you, Celia. What's wrong with you?"

Son of a gun, I thought. I'd done it again. I'd upset my Drew. I watched the creases in his face deepen. I watched his eyes get colder and more tangled. Ever since we'd married my husband had taken on the aspect of an avuncular elder whenever he spoke to me. His comparative maturity—he was eleven years older—put me at a constant disadvantage. He could always say he'd experienced more of life and he'd always be right.

"So why were you late again?" Drew said. "Tonight what's your excuse?"

You need to understand. Drew never once hit me. He only pushed me. Or held me down. Or wrapped his arms around me, not lovingly but therapeutically, to get me to see his side of things. He never raised his voice. He scolded gently. The scolding began on our wedding night, after the party, and after we were home together, when the two of us were entirely alone. That's when my new husband began to list the ways I had disappointed him ever since the day we'd met. The list was long. Mostly it consisted of his diligent observations of those times, in his eyes, when I had flirted with other men, and women, too, and made a fool out of him. He'd made a mental note of all the times. He had collected those times like glass on a beach. Men in checkout lines at the grocery store. Bartenders. Next-door neighbors. Anyone who wasn't Drew himself. The mailman. The coat-check girl. The trash man. The waitress. The newspaper boy. It was news to me. Was there something salacious about the way I looked at people in general? Did I smile in an inappropriate and flirtatious way? Was there something seductive about the way I dressed? Did I think sexual thoughts more often than your average girl of that era? "You're just a slut, I guess," Drew said. "But you'll learn." I began to cry. "Go ahead and cry," Drew said. I cried harder. I didn't mean to. It was a ridiculous situation. We were newlyweds, and it was our wedding night, but my body felt the need to get away from him. I tried to leave the usual way, through the front door.

Drew wouldn't let me. I learned the true meaning of the verb *to strong-arm.* Whenever I took a step toward the door Drew shoved me back with the heel of his hand. It wasn't a blow. It felt neutral, not violent. The shock of it, though—to have someone's hand on my chest, shoving me back, again, and again—left me feeling dazed and incredulous. It was like fighting sea waves. Drew was inexhaustible. He wasn't enjoying himself but the lesson needed to be learned and he was my grim teacher.

I changed tactics and ran away, into our bedroom, where I locked the door behind me.

I felt Drew standing on the other side.

"Where can you go?" he said.

His tone was reasonable. His voice was gentle. I'd show him. I'd climb out the window. As I have mentioned, it was a ridiculous situation, almost funny. There I was, climbing out a bedroom window of my own house while wearing the sexy nightgown I'd bought for our wedding night. The windowsill was weathered. When I straddled it, long splinters dug into my thighs. It was a five-foot drop to the ground and I twisted my ankle when I landed. In bare feet I limped across the road. Would he chase me down? I'd learn, later, that was not his way. The windows of the neighbors' houses stared out blankly. It was past midnight by then, and the thought of waking anyone, or asking anyone to help me out of my ridiculous situation, felt shameful. Also, let's be honest: What had Drew done to me? He hadn't hit me. His tone had remained reasonable throughout. I limped through a stand of trees until I came to the neighborhood playground, a patch of the world I'd loved as a child. I sat down on a swing. I sat a long time. My mind was empty. I swayed back and forth. After a while, I went home.

The way I'd come home again, tonight.

Drew flipped his burgers.

"Are you ready to tell me why you were late?" he said.

"I'm sorry," I said. "I missed the early train."

"Now you're going to cry," he said.

Drew was correct. Tears came to my eyes. That's the way it was between us. Whenever Drew predicted I was about to cry, I would fall into a tearful panic. And whenever we came to this inevitable place in any given conversation, I could never be sure if he was about to hold me down for my own good, or if he was about to give me the cold shoulder.

"I'm going out," Drew said.

Cold shoulder, then.

Drew tossed his burger-flipping spatula into the sink and left. I heard a door slam. I heard his car start up. The sound of the motor faded and disappeared. I turned off the stove. I stood and ate those burgers straight from the pan. I let the juice drip down my chin. I wondered how long the cold shoulder treatment was going to last this time. The last time he didn't speak to me for a good three weeks. It began when I'd asked Drew if he'd be interested in lasciviously sipping a drop of wine from my navel. "That's disgusting, Celia," he'd said. "I can't believe you want me to do such a disgusting thing!" Drinking a drop of wine from my navel wasn't even a thing that sounded so sexy to me to begin with. I'd read about it in a *Cosmo* article called "Ten Flirty Tips to Up Your Game in Bed." I was thinking Drew and I could try something that stretched us. Maybe it would help me warm up to the idea of sexual congress with my husband, an activity I had never much enjoyed. Sometimes I just wanted Drew to hold my hand. Whenever I asked him to hold my hand, though, he would say no, because the intimate things we did together always needed to be his idea.

After I ate those burgers I cleaned up the kitchen and then I took a shower. After my shower I found some cardboard and electrician's tape and patched up the broken window of my mother's Oldsmobile. I was pleased with the job I'd done. It looked neat and tidy, as if I'd been patching up broken windows all my life.

When I came back inside I spent some time with my Barbie doll collection, in the pantry, arranging the boxes in a way that pleased me. Then I watched TV. I felt so stupid. What was the matter with me? What? Drew's accusatory question kept echoing in my head. Vivienne Bianco was dead. I'd told Drew the entire tragic story with gleeful abandon. I'd romanticized her bloody end. Vivienne's story felt like a television show to me. I tried to go to sleep but I couldn't sleep. I kept trying to think about poor Vivienne as a real person and not as a TV actress. I tried to put myself in her situation and to imagine a man like Gene Bianco coming toward me—a man who meant to do me grave harm—but I couldn't. I was still awake when Drew came home and pulled me by my ankles into the middle of the bed, and left my legs dangling over. That was the first night I remember feeling that glorious feeling, the one I have already mentioned to you, of leaving my body and flying up, up into the air, like a muscular swan: rapacious, radiant, and free.

The next morning the sunlight came blazing through the bedroom window like warm honey-scotch. I didn't get up right away. I stayed in bed, ruminating. I gazed at my husband's sleeping slack face. My husband never raised his voice. My husband was patient, he was kind, he did not envy, he did not boast, he was not proud, and he played kickball on our street with all the neighborhood kids. My husband did more than his share of chores. He remembered when to buy new toothbrushes. In that brash and golden morning light my husband's sleeping face looked like a marble statue, carved by an angel. I was filled with gratefulness for the way he had come home to me the night before. He had made love to me. I figured it meant he'd forgiven me. And all these many years later, as I'm telling you a story about a nineteen-year-old girl who thought she was in love with her husband, I begin to ask myself a question or two. For instance. Has it already crossed the girl's mind back on that gorgeous, sun-dazzle morning, as she gazes at her husband's tranquil sleeping face, that she wants him dead? It has not crossed that girl's mind. Not once. Not in a million years. Not until later that same day, at least. Just at this moment the girl can't imagine a future will ever come in which she will feel the compulsion to take out her mother's old nail file from her secret stash of memory-objects and bury it deep inside her husband's ear. Not one of her swirling confused excited thoughts about *love and death* has coalesced into a plan of any kind. But one thing is true about the girl on that dazzle-bright day: Her body has already begun to fight back. Sometimes in the middle of the night her body flings an arm out in her husband's direction. The arm will clock the husband hard on the nose, or in the groin area. The husband will shake the girl roughly to wake her, and he'll complain about how she's "done it again." How can he blame his wife when she's so clearly been fast asleep? Even the husband will concede that she is not to blame. And if you had asked the girl back on that honey-scotch morning whether she felt any feeling for that man other than an abiding, grateful love, she would have denied it.

THREE

ELEVEN MINUTES TO SPARE

So when *did* I first fall in love with my Drew? I can tell you exactly. It happened on the day he first invited me to the beach. I'd known Drew for three weeks by then. I kept seeing him around at the hospital. He seemed nice. Whenever my mother needed to stay overnight he would come by her room in the morning with flowers from the gift shop and my mother would say, "Don't let this one go, Celia! He's a keeper!" and the two of them would share a chuckle or two. But it didn't mean anything. The flowers Drew gave my mother were past their prime. They were drooping and brown and would have been thrown out by afternoon if Drew hadn't rescued them. I still thought it was a thoughtful gesture on his part, but what my mother said about Drew being a keeper made no sense to me, because he was too old for me.

After my mother was discharged she invited Drew over for lunch, to thank him for his many kindnesses to her while she was in the hospital. It was just sandwiches, but she put a lot of effort into it, and when lunch was over she and Drew got to talking about this and that, and about the fine weather, and then Drew said he was driving over to the coast that afternoon and would love our company and my mother said, "Drew, what a tease you are, you know I'm not well enough for a big adventure like that, but how about taking my girl? She never goes out anywhere if she can help it, these days," and that was that.

The beach was only six miles from Redwood City but it always felt far away because it was hidden by a line of hills and after I rode up those hills and came down the other side I always felt as if I'd crossed over into a foreign land. The sky was always white. The sun was always bigger than elsewhere on the planet. When Drew and I crested the hill that afternoon I saw a sea of clouds spread beneath us like a cotton quilt, and then we descended through the clouds and I saw the shimmering Pacific. When we got to the coast road, Drew turned south. We drove past fields of giant artichokes, and fields full of grass, and I remember seeing horses running, and feeling as free and easy as one of those horses, where for a second or two I could forget about my mother and how sick she was.

Drew drove all the way to Santa Cruz, a quaint coastal town with a boardwalk full of amusements. He said he wanted to take me on the roller coaster. I said I didn't mind. After the roller coaster he took me to Fosters Freeze, and after we had burgers and shakes I thought we were walking back to the car but Drew led me elsewhere by the elbow, to a two-story motel, where he'd reserved a room for us. That was the big surprise he'd had in store for me. I told myself I must have given him a certain impression. That I'd suggested my willingness. Also, he'd prepaid for the room. We were both living with our mothers at the time and it was a special treat for us to have some private time, he told me. The walls of the room were painted blue and the curtains were drawn. I remember how it felt so dark in that room after walking through the bright-sun afternoon just outside the door. We stood there awhile. Drew kissed me for the first time. His kiss was startling on account of all the unexpected tongue in my mouth. It seemed important to act as if I liked his kiss, though, and when it was over, I smiled.

"I will always take care of you," he said.

"Okay," I said.

"May I?" he said.

I nodded. I did that. Drew unbuttoned the first button on my shirt. A short while later I was naked. I can't say I hated it. I felt trembly and on the brink of big feelings, and maybe I felt helpless, too, and unable to voice an opinion about what was going to happen next, but I wasn't scared. There was a sweet pulsing ache between my legs. I thought whatever happened next was probably something I'd already agreed to, by allowing him to undress me.

"So you're not a natural blonde," he said.

This comment caught me off guard. Because I was a natural blonde. Just not down there. When I was a kid my hair had been so blonde it was nearly white. Before Drew said that thing about me not being a natural blonde, I'd never thought about the color of my hair down there. I'd never known it was meant to be the same color as the hair on my head. This new knowledge, about something that was at once so intimate and so obvious about my body, distressed me. I felt weak and weepy, and mortified by the way my body had betrayed me by growing the wrong-colored hair down there. "I'm sorry," I said. I felt so sorry for the way I'd let Drew down. To keep myself from crying, I closed my eyes. I felt Drew's hand between my legs. He was covering my shamefully wrong-colored hair with his hand. He was signaling to me that he was still willing to touch me there, in spite of his disappointment. And I felt so grateful. His hand on my body felt so good to me. It really did. He began to move his fingers back and forth, and then he said: "Look at me," and I opened my eyes. His face was so close. "Do you like that?" he said, and I nodded. "Won't you lie down on the bed?" he said next, and I laid myself down on the bed with my legs dangling over. I watched him take off his shoes and socks. Next he took off his trousers and his boxers. He folded his trousers and his boxers neatly and put them on the chair by the window. He kept his shirt on. He walked back to the bed. He stood there awhile, looking at me. I didn't look at his privates. I looked away. I wanted to give his privates their privacy. What happened next was fumbly and embarrassing and I didn't know what to do and then he was inside me. Plow and plow and plow and plow. Push and push. Push and plow. It wasn't painful, but it hurt. His lovemaking was so uncomfortable. It was hard for me to get a good breath. I felt so inadequate. I felt so bad at lovemaking. He seemed distracted and unhappy. I wondered if it was my fault.

"I feel like I'm swimming," he said.

So it *was* my fault. It was because I wasn't tight enough. It was because I had a slack purse. It was because I was a lousy lay. When had my purse gotten slack? What had I done wrong in life, to be so slack down there? To tell the truth, I felt tight and dry. He'd kept on plowing me for so long that I felt like I had a sore throat, only down there. I could tell Drew was proud of his self-control, but I felt rotten, like I wasn't lovely enough or tight enough to give him release. As for my own release, the notion of feeling any sexual pleasure, when I was so worried about him and whether I made him happy, made it hard for me to think about what I was feeling, and he never asked, and then he was done.

There was no blood on the sheet.

"So you're not a virgin," he said.

But I was. Or had been.

Let him say something beautiful to me, I prayed.

"You're mine now," he said.

He was smiling like a child who has just used the potty for the first time, or maybe like a child who has just learned for the first time how to write his name, in big block letters. And he had written his name upon my body. Oh yes, my dears. And I had welcomed him to do it. I had wanted him to do it. And I didn't want this man to feel any other feeling than love, for me. And so I covered both of our bodies over with the damp sheet. I lay my head on his sweaty shoulder. I wrapped myself in a glorious love story, one I would tell myself over and over again. In this story, my Drew was a man who would always take care of me.

I loved him. I really did.

"I love you," I said.

The morning after I'd made the mistake of telling Drew about Vivienne Bianco's bloody fate, I woke up so early that I caught the first train of the day. The train car was nearly empty that time of day. All of us passengers had been thrown together by circumstance and I wondered what sort of lives these other people led. Across from me was an elderly humped woman who had dyed her hair a brilliant electric red. It's a color you don't see anymore because it came from a bottle of a long-discontinued grocery-store brand. She was looking out the window and sighing and touching her lips as we traveled along, as if reliving in her mind an urgent tryst from the night before, and it seems a shame to me now that I didn't say hello to her that day. She probably had some stories to tell. The rest of us in the car were dull everyday sorts of people. Most of us were dozing. Seeing those dozing faces in the train car with me reminded me of how tired I was, and I closed my eyes. A few people were making small talk, albeit in a tired morning way, and their voices drifted into my thoughts, and then my dreams.

My daughter's orthodontic bills are going to bankrupt us
No wine better than Gallo
No one's calling you fat
Let's get takeout tonight
Our girl thinks she's in love

Poor ninny can't see the dangers right in front of her
Can't see the signs
Hey, girl. You've got to buy those knives
Celia
Celia
Celia!

Then I heard a good hard screeching of the brakes, and opened my eyes. Everyone was already standing in the aisle, ready to get to where they needed to be. I joined them. We shuffled out. The big clock in the station said half-past-six. I had ninety minutes to spare before I needed to be at my workstation. I walked slowly. I exalted in the fresh new morning. The air was so still that I could hear the satellites passing overhead. All at once I found myself standing in front of the building where I worked. By habit my feet had delivered me there. I told myself not to go in yet. I still had time. Then I heard a gurgly voice next to my ear, telling me to go inside. It happens sometimes. A voice will come crying out of the silence and deliver a message meant just for me. Maybe you hear voices, too. Maybe you're hearing my voice right now in your head. At any rate, in my case that gurgly voice said to me, *Wouldn't it be nice to grab a doughnut and a cup of coffee before work starts for the day?*—and so I went in, and I rode the elevator to the fourth-floor cafeteria, where Meena, from the second floor, happened to be in line just ahead of me.

"Celia!" Meena said. "How about that Randall Smiley?"

"How about that Randall Smiley," I agreed.

Meena nodded in a knowing way. I nodded back. We scooted our yellow trays along. I could tell that Meena had been deeply affected by Randall's story from the day before because she was wearing a yellow suit and her blouse was tastefully cream-colored. I wasn't sure if Meena had purposefully adopted the fashion choices of the dead Vivienne Bianco, or if it was more of a subliminal impulse on her part, but I was too shy to call attention to her clothes by asking her this question, and so I picked out a jelly doughnut from the doughnut row and put it on my tray. When I came to the five-gallon percolator I poured myself a coffee. My choices—the doughnut, the coffee—felt deliberate and consequential, instead of ordinary and everyday, because Meena was watching me. She waited for me as I paid the cashier. Then she invited me to follow her over to a big table where three other second-floor girls were already boisterously gathered.

"Girls! This is Celia from the third floor!" Meena announced.

"We all know Celia!" one of them said, and laughed.

They were all jolly second-floor girls who worked together in the New Accounts Center, which was a very different place from the Resident Billing Office. In the New Accounts Center, the girls were busy hooking up new telephones for people all day. It was a happy place. Customers calling into the New Accounts Center were grateful, not bitter. They were excited to learn what their brand-new phone numbers were going to be. The workers on the first and second and third floors of the phone company all meshed like the gears of a finely tuned pocket watch. On the first floor was the payment office, where customers came in to pay their phone bills after I'd ripped their lips. Once the customers paid their bills, they could use the phone banks in the lobby to call up to the second-floor girls, who had the power to turn the phone service back on, and then the second-floor girls called me on the third floor, in the billing office, to let me know the bill had been paid, so I could make a note of it. We were talking back and forth all the livelong day. That's why I knew these women's names but not their faces. Tammy. Joan. Helen. They introduced themselves around the table. Their faces resembled their names to a surprising degree. There was enough room for Meena and me to squeeze in, and we did. Meena slathered some grape jelly on her toast and took a big bite. Her teeth were large. She was a big-boned gal and her blouse was too small in front and there was a gap between the middle two buttons where a patch of pale freckled skin peeked through.

"You're so young, Celia," she declared, while chewing.

"Nineteen," I said.

"You look younger," Tammy said.

The second-floor girls looked at me appraisingly.

"You look about fourteen," Tammy said. "For real, I mean."

"Not that you know how to use it," Meena said. "You dress like my grandma."

I said my mother had made all my clothes, which was just the truth. They looked at me sympathetically. They did not want to criticize clothes my own mother had made, maybe.

"Seems the Farter was calling in again all day yesterday," Joan said out of the blue.

"The Farter!" Tammy said. "The Farter called my line yesterday, too! I swear, that man waits for the gas to build up and be ready to burst out of him before he calls in!"

Their laughter turned to snorts. I understood them. Anyone with an itch to speak with another human being could dial into the phone company any time they pleased and get one of us on the line and we were a captive audience because, unless customers were threatening or obscene, we weren't supposed to transfer them to our floor supervisors. We had Jesus Christs calling in all the time. We had Patty Hearsts and Richard Nixons. I'd never heard of the Farter, though.

"I swear, he holds the receiver down there!" Tammy said. "Right where his message will come through loud and clear! He's a serial farter!"

"Poor Celia," Joan said. "What must she think of us?"

"I bet Celia could tell us some stories," Meena said. "People calling into the billing office are always full of stories and excuses."

I boldly told those girls a story about Mrs. Robert Brisket's son's addiction to phone porno.

"You should have passed that boy onto Meena before you ripped his lips," Joan said. "Meena has a phone-porno side business. How much do you make in a week, Meena?"

"Plenty," Meena said. "A man will pay up the kaboodle for good and lively sex talk."

"We're unholy degenerates," Joan said. "Poor Celia!"

"Poor Celia!" Tammy said.

"I don't know why, but I am feeling very tenderly toward our poor Celia," Meena said. "I feel like she could use a friend. I like you, Celia. I really do. You should come out with us second-floor girls after work sometime, for winks and drinks."

"I'm married," I said.

"What's that got to do with the price of beef?" Joan said.

"How about that Vivienne Bianco?" Tammy said, changing the subject.

"Poor Vivienne," I said.

"Oh no, Celia, no," Meena said. "Not poor *Vivienne.* What you mean is, poor *Randall.* Vivienne Bianco had it coming. She'd been psychologically torturing her husband for years. She'd reduced him to pitiful putty. She was using Randall as yet another way to get back at him. But Randall caught on. He was trying to get away from her. He really was. She threatened to get him fired if he ever left her. And now this mess lands in his lap, with a murder, and a trial, and everything, and he's lost his job anyway—"

"But Randall told us it was really love," I said.

"Oh, you sweet girl, it wasn't ever really love," Meena said. "Sure, that's what Randall wanted it to be. He was in love in the beginning. Vivienne led him on. It wasn't ever really love on her part. Randall told me the whole terrible story."

"When did Randall tell you the whole terrible story?" I said.

"Randall's hiding out at Meena's place on account of Gene Bianco being an Italian," Joan said. "Randall figures the Mob is probably after him now."

"Sounds far-fetched," Tammy said. "Not every Italian is a mobster. Are they?"

"Maybe Randall planned it all," Helen said.

Helen had been so quiet up to then. She was a small woman made smaller by the way she sat. She was completely forgettable. That is why I'd nearly forgotten I'd seen her the day before, in the designated break room for smokers. She'd heard the same story I'd heard, from Randall's own lips, and now a new idea had caught up with her.

"Think about it," Helen said. "Let's say Randall Smiley is

tired of being played for a fool. He wants to get rid of Vivienne Bianco once and for all. Let's say Vivienne has told Randall all about her husband's jealous rages. So Randall comes up with a plan. He starts leaving his brand of cigarette butts in Vivienne's ashtrays. He leaves his wristwatch behind somewhere in the house where Gene is sure to find it. He leaves two dozen anonymous messages at Gene's tractor company, all about Vivienne's adulterous ways. He cleverly changes his voice each time. Before long Gene is convinced the whole town is laughing at him. He thinks his only option is to murder his wife in a fit of jealous rage. And, voilà. Randall has solved his Vivienne problem for good, and he's done it in a way that leaves him entirely blameless!"

"Quite the story, Helen," Meena said.

"Randall Smiley might just be an evil genius," Helen said.

"Huh," I said. I caught myself thinking that Helen was probably right, and that Randall Smiley was probably an evil genius. I'm persuadable that way.

"I just can't imagine Randall Smiley as an evil genius," Tammy said. "It's unimaginable."

"Evil geniuses like to come across as cheerful bumblers," Helen said. "They are always people you would never suspect."

"Ah," Tammy said.

"Finally the day comes for the coup de grâce," Helen said. "Randall leaves the used condom on the floor in plain sight *on purpose.* He knows the sight of that condom will enrage the husband past the point of no return. His plan goes off without a hitch."

"Shut up, Helen," Meena said.

"The only way it could have worked out better for Randall Smiley is if he'd somehow figured out how to get Gene Bianco to kill himself, too, in a fit of grief and remorse," Helen said. "Then Randall wouldn't need to testify at the trial. That would have been an evil genius move for sure!"

"You don't know a thing about it, Helen," Meena said.

"What do you know about it, Meena?" I said.

"Meena knows plenty," Joan said. "She's practically dating Randall Smiley these days."

This news, that Meena was practically dating Randall Smiley, and not just providing him with a secret hideaway to keep him safe from the Mob, was so startling that my mind filled up at once with a hundred blinking stars.

"What of it, Joan?" Meena said. "You date your *customers*."

"Why shouldn't I?" Joan said. "Sometimes a customer's voice attracts me. Sometimes I decide to meet him after work. I tell the guy to hold a red carnation. The carnation gives me a chance to check him out before he knows who I am."

"You're crazy," Meena said. "One day, you're gonna get yourself killed."

"Look who's talking," Joan said. "Look who's dating a man whose last girlfriend ended up dead. Anyhow, I guess we all do it. Talk back to our customers, I mean. I like to find out what my customers can give me other than a hard time. What about you, Celia? I'll bet you've had a flirty conversation with one of your customers a time or two!"

The second-floor girls looked in my direction. I couldn't answer Joan's question, because my mouth was full of doughnut and my mind was full of blinking stars. It had never once entered my head to strike up a flirty conversation with a customer. For one thing, I was married. For another thing, people calling into the billing office to make payment arrangements were by definition on life's losing side. Also the floor supervisors could listen in on our calls anytime. In spite of these cold facts, I was intrigued. I wanted to ask Joan some questions of my own. But by then it was six minutes to eight and we all got up and rushed toward the elevator bay.

There was such a crowd waiting there for the elevator that I changed my mind and took the fire stairs down to the third floor. All of us billing operators were hustling to our seats and adjusting our headsets. In that rustling bustle Randall's workstation, six rows over, looked empty and forlorn. As I waited for the floor supervisor to flip the call switch open, the way he did each day precisely at eight o'clock, I thought about Randall and Meena. I guessed from the look in Meena's eye whenever she had mentioned his name that Randall wasn't sleeping on Meena's couch. Sometimes people amazed me. In the wake of Randall's deadly illicit encounter with murder and sex, he and Meena had found each other. Together they had stepped forward fearlessly, straight into the next chapter of their lives—no need to wait for the dust to settle, move on, move on!—and how I envied them! How I marveled at the way those two had unburdened themselves from any need to grieve, or to feel shame, or to wait for a sober day or two at least before beginning their urgent new love story together! Before the year was out those two would quit the phone company. They would start a new business, making smut films in Meena's garage with themselves as the stars. They named their upstart business "Mean Doll Pictures," a clever mash-up of both their names. They'd make a deal with the owners of an old drive-in theater out in the East Bay to show their pictures every night. Drive-in theaters had mostly gone belly-up by then. Porn was their salvation. I have long since lost track of Meena and Randall. I never got to hear how Randall extricated himself from under Vivienne Bianco's blood-soaked bed. I still think about him, though, and I still envy him for the way he sprang back so quickly from the tragic loss of his illicit lover. Oh yes, my dears.

But hold on.

I was telling you a completely different part of this story, about when I was nineteen, and it was 1974, and the seconds were ticking past fast and faster until eight o'clock arrived.

The floor supervisor flipped the call switch.

My call light lit up.

"This is Celia. How can I help you?" I said.

I heard a pause.

You can hear a pause, you know. I knew this pause. It happened when someone was about to say something I didn't want to hear.

"I'm watching you, Celia," a voice said.

"Drew?" I said.

I thought it was probably Drew's voice in my ear, on that first call of the day. My husband liked to call into the Resident Billing Office like that, anonymously, to make sure I wasn't playing hooky from work to go off on a salacious adventure with somebody who wasn't him. The caller hung up before I could be sure. Maybe it was a prank call and nothing more. Maybe it wasn't Drew. I knew from experience that if I went home and said to Drew: "Did you call me at work again?" he would deny it. Maybe with reason, and maybe not. "Why would I call you at work?" he'd say. "I get too much of you at home as it is."

Maybe it was Drew and maybe it wasn't, but either way that first call of the day put me on edge for the rest of the morning. Every time I said, *This is Celia, how can I help you?*, I kept expecting to hear the same low growl of a voice, telling me to watch out. The morning stumbled forward. The voices poured into my ear. Somebody wanted a new phone installed, and I transferred her down to the second floor. Somebody asked for an extra week's grace to pay the bill—no problem. I didn't have any of those unpleasantly dramatic sorts of calls, thank goodness, where someone decided to yell at me or to curse or to cry or to tell me I was a "bitch" or a "cunt" for disconnecting their telephone, but I kept expecting something like that to happen, and expectation can be almost as bad as the real thing. Every call I answered seemed poised to transform itself into a threat.

By the time my lunch break came around I was exhausted and on edge. I took the elevator to the cafeteria and ordered a grilled cheese sammie and I looked around for the second-floor girls but they did not appear. I ate three bites of my sammie and stuffed the rest in the trash and went out for a stroll. The day had turned gray and sullen. There must have been a conference of accountants at the Moscone Center because the streets were crowded with young professionals. Their starched way of existing in this world depressed me. I turned down a side street, and then another one, until the crowdedness of the sidewalks petered out and I was alone and walking along a narrow alley somewhere down by the Embarcadero. I couldn't see the bay but I could tell it was near because of the seagull cries. I stopped walking for some reason when I found myself standing directly in front of one of those old pawn shops, the sort you don't see anymore. The window was crammed full of ceramic trinkets and antique muskets. It was so full of dusty stuff that it took me a while to notice a man inside the shop, looking out at me. The man's mustache was enormous. He was smoking a cigar with gusto. He gestured with his cigar for me to come on in. I had a disparaging opinion of pawn shops. My feeling was that pawn shops were places of poverty and desperation and last chances. On the other hand it felt as if I'd been drawn to that pawn shop by an invisible compulsion that I couldn't resist, and so I opened the door.

A bell tinkled.

That cigar-smoking mustachioed gentleman was the only one in there.

"Howdy," he said. "What're you looking for today, young lady?"

"I'm looking for a knife," I said. "Do you have any of those?"

My own words took me aback. I had no interest in knives or in buying knives.

But the man seemed to think my knife-quest was only natural.

"What kind of knife?" he said. "Chef's knife? Parer? Bread knife? Cleaver?"

Cleaver had a ring to it. But not quite the right ring.

"None of those," I said.

"Aha," he said. "I also have utility knives. Hunting knives. Pocketknives. How about this one?"

He took a mass of keys from his pocket and found a key and used it to open the glass case in front of him, and he picked up one of those little red Swiss Army knives with all the gadgets.

"This one has it all," he said. "Very handy. Toothpick. Screwdriver. Corkscrew. Bottle opener. Small scissors."

As he named each of these handy little tools, he pulled them out from their hidden places, one by one, and he set out a green velvet cloth on the counter and put the knife on top of it.

"Along with the two blades, of course," he said. "One serrated. One straight."

That clever pocketknife was not at all what I wanted. It looked like a disemboweled thing lying there on the green velvet cloth. But the man was so eager, and so sure he had solved the puzzle of me and my knife needs, that I bent down and examined it respectfully for several seconds before I straightened up again and shook my head.

"Not this one," I said.

"Maybe something simpler, for everyday carry?" he said.

"Something light and versatile? To be stored in a purse, or worn on a string around the neck? Very handy in a pinch. You'd be surprised how handy a small blade for everyday carry can be."

"What about a dirk?" I said. "Do you have any of those?"

He reconsidered me.

"Yes, we do have one of those," he said.

He led me to a different glass case and unlocked it.

"This here dirk is the real deal," he said. "The blade is thirteen inches. That's long enough to pierce the heart and come out the other side."

There it was. One big old knife. I hadn't known before that dirks were as long as thirteen inches. It looked more sword than knife. When I'd asked to see a dirk, I'd pictured something like those cunning switchblades I'd seen in the movie *West Side Story*. This was something else. The blade was a dusky-steel color. That knife gave me a feeling it had pierced many a heart in its day. The handle was made from bone, or maybe antler.

"Hmm," I said.

"Not entirely legal to carry it concealed," the man said.

He said it as if illegality was an asset when it came to knives, and that knowing this one was not entirely legal to carry, concealed, might sway me into buying it.

"There is a matching smaller blade," he said. "It's a lovely pair."

He took out a smaller knife. It had a matching handle. Antler, or bone.

"This here is what you call a *black knife*," he said. "In Scottish parlance, that's *sgian dubh*. Traditionally the dirk is worn on the side, and the black knife is worn in the boot."

I'd fallen for that little black knife already. Don't ask me why.

"Quite a handy knife," he said. "The two make a handsome pair, don't you agree?"

"I certainly do," I said.

"You're Scottish, I take it?"

"Could be," I said.

"Shopping for the man in your life? Is he a collector?"

"Something like that."

"I have more blades in back."

"I'll take the little one," I said.

"I will not sell these beauties separately," he said indignantly. "Just as the pair."

He began to chew on his nub of a leftover cigar with extra verve while I reconsidered the dirk. It was formidable. It scared me a little. But maybe I could learn to love that dirk if I gave it half a chance. Just as I probably would have learned to love my dad, named Dirk, if I'd been given half the chance. I thought about my dad, and about all the mysteries surrounding the paternal side of the family. How strange to have had a mother who was obsessed with sewing things together, and a father who was named for a weapon that tore things apart. A time to sew, a time to rend. I thought it poetic. I thought it might explain why my parents had split up. I didn't know if my dad was dead or alive but I'd come to the doughy conclusion, by then, that owning a dirk might be a way for my dad and me to psychically connect, no matter what astral realm he might currently be inhabiting. This knife and my dad glued themselves together in my thoughts until it seemed obvious to me that by rejecting the dirk I would be rejecting my father. I was fated to buy that pair of knives, together, and not just the small darling one all on its own. By buying these knives, I'd grow closer in spirit to my dad. It made perfect sense. It was meant to happen. We agreed on a price with barely a haggle. At the last minute I picked out a canvas gym bag that said SPORT on its side, from a big bin of gym bags, and suitcases, and briefcases, and purses and pocketbooks. With my new sport bag I could carry my knives discreetly through the streets of San Francisco and all the way back to the office instead of marching along like Joan of Arc without the chain mail. I left that pawn shop feeling ready for any contingency. Time was behaving strangely that afternoon. I was certain I'd been on my pawn shop adventure for an hour or a week but I got back to the office with eleven minutes to spare.

FOUR

LONG-LEGGED CRABS

As soon as I stepped through the big glass doors and into the lobby, I heard a voice calling my name in a plaintive lonely bleat: "—Celia? Celia? Celia?—Do you know Celia?—Can you tell me where to find Celia?—Where is Celia?—Are you Celia?"—and when I turned my head toward the sound of my name, a pair of eyes instantly found me in the crowd, because everyone else was rushing past, and then somebody—me, that is—had heard her name being called and had responded by turning her head. A woman was walking toward me. She looked so sad. There was something about her gait that filled me with the wish to console. On the other hand I didn't know her. She had been calling out my name for some reason or another, and she was shuffling toward me, and then she was standing in front of me and looking at me in a confused, possibly threatening way. She was wearing one of those stylish trench coats with the deep pockets, the kind that everyone wore back then, even on days when it wasn't raining. She was both tall and severe. She was tall enough and severe enough to look down on nearly everyone, including me. But there was something soft about her, too. A resignation in her eyes. Her eyes were pale. Her hair looked as if somebody had cut it with a pair of hedge clippers.

"Celia," she said.

I might have nodded.

"Celia? Maybe you remember me? Mrs. Robert Brisket? We spoke yesterday?"

"I need to get back to work," I said.

Mrs. Brisket reached out and held on to my arm. She was leaning toward me in a way that reminded me of a sad willow tree. I pulled my arm away from her twiglike fingers. I took a step back.

"Please, Celia," she said.

"I can't help you," I said.

"Please," she said again. "You don't understand—"

"People are always telling me I don't understand," I said.

I sounded colder than I wanted to. But she frightened me a little. Typically we billing operators don't ever meet our customers face-to-face. There's too much at stake. It's an emotional thing to have your lips ripped. People tend to hate us. I needed to get away. I felt like calling out for help but everyone was rushing by.

"Mrs. Brisket," I said. "You can use the phone bank over there to call into the office and make payment arrangements. Then you pay over at that window. That's the payment office. That's how it's done. I can't forgive your bill in the middle of the lobby. The money is owed."

"Please," she said. "If his father finds out—"

"I'm sorry," I said.

I could have told Mrs. Brisket that when it comes to phone porno it's usually the husband who is the culprit, not the child. The wives are in denial. In those days, men needed to make do with dial-up voice porno recorded on scratchy tapes, because the phone was all there was. Mrs. Brisket kept looking at me through her cornflower eyes. Everything was in motion in that cavernous lobby except for Mrs. Brisket and me. People were scurrying from here to there. The space was busy with hard-echo footsteps, and brittle voices, and bright thoughts, all of them bouncing off the marble walls. Then the world muffled itself and I heard a voice next to my ear, as clearly as if I'd been wearing my headset upstairs and was listening to the next call in the queue, and the voice said: *One day this woman is going to do you a tremendous favor*—and then the world turned on its axis another notch or two, and the words I'd imagined had been meant for me alone were nothing but a misheard echo bouncing from the walls, and here was Mrs. Robert Brisket, bending and drooping in my direction.

"You're a terrible person," she said.

In those days a job at the phone company was the elephant graveyard of jobs. The phone company was the place you worked until you died. I'd gotten the job after a hospice volunteer had come to visit my mother, and had learned of my plight, that I was about to be orphaned at seventeen. "Your daughter will have benefits for life!" the hospice volunteer had promised my poor dying mom. "A good solid job! No one ever quits the phone company, it's like one big family! I can put in a good word!" And before I knew it I was a phone company girl. I often wished I'd landed on the first floor, in the payment office, or on the second floor, where most of the girls were in their twenties and therefore closer to my age, instead of in the Resident Billing Office, where most of the girls were old, and had arthritis, and burgeoning hips, and grandchildren. Or better yet I could have worked in the executive offices on the fifth and sixth floors. When people called to speak with my boss I'd tell them he was in an important meeting. I'd wear nice clothes. The only place I would have liked less than the third floor was the fourth-floor cafeteria, but being a third-floor girl was almost as bad. To work in the Resident Billing Office was to live in a fractious sea of contradiction. We were supposed to be kind to our customers but also to rip their lips if they didn't pay up. There was a constant civil war going on between the compassionate ones among us and the vicious lip rippers among us, and I'd yet to settle fully into one faction or the other, either the rippers or the redeemers. I wanted to be a good person but sometimes a feeling would come over me and I'd rip lips all the livelong day. Then I'd feel ashamed of myself. That's why I thought Mrs. Brisket was probably right. I was probably a terrible person. Even my husband said so. Even my mother had said so, before the shadows got her. By the time I was done thinking through all these things Mrs. Brisket had let go of my arm. I could see for myself that the fight had gone out of her. She looked like a spent balloon. She'd given up on me. She let me walk away. As I stood waiting for the next elevator to come along I glanced back just in time to see Mrs. Brisket shuffling out through the big glass doors. Once outside she jaywalked in a meandering manner, making the cars honk and swerve before she made it safely to the other side. Now that she was safely over there across the street, I felt sorry for her again. Then the elevator came and I stepped in and forgot about her.

Upstairs I plugged in just in time. I looked over at the emptiness of Randall Smiley's workstation six rows away. His absence felt like the death of a distant relative I'd always meant to get to know and now it was too late. I would never know what had happened to Randall after he found himself hiding a mattress-width away from a grief-crazed killer while trying to suppress a sneeze that might mean his doom. I'd never know what ghosts haunted Randall Smiley still. My days would be duller than before. And because it was that kind of day, the first customer I found in my ear, after I'd set my headset on my head, was the customer who was my biggest fan.

All of us operators had our biggest fans. We collected fans like whales collect barnacles. People would call in and ask for us by name and think we were friends. Or sometimes people would call in over and over again until they got their favorite operator on the line by the luck of the draw. I called one fan of mine Mr. Willy. Later, I would learn his real name—Lester Krebs—and you might have heard of him because he was in all the newspapers, later—but at the time he was just Mr. Willy to me. He would keep dialing into the billing office until Celia, aka Operator 737, was the one who answered.

"This is Celia, how can I help you?" I'd say.

"Celia! Is that my Celia?" Mr. Willy would say. He sounded like a man who has crossed the desert in the hopes of finding his Celia waiting for him on the other side with a pitcher of water and a loving bosom. "Celia, oh, my Celia!" he'd say, and then he'd gasp a small gasp and say: "Oh, please, Celia, please, I need you to put a sock on my willy! Can't you do that for me? My willy is so lonely and so cold! Can't you put your tight little sock on my willy, sweetheart?"

Mr. Willy's questions used to shock me, but no longer. When I didn't answer, I'd hear another agonized little gasp. It wasn't a pornographic gasp, or a masturbatory gasp. I had plenty of experience with those. They came with the job. Mr. Willy's gasp was more like an encounter with loneliness, or maybe, like an encounter with a desire so pure that it broke the bonds of semantic meaning and all the man could do was babble on about socks. Mr. Willy's desire reached through the telephone wires and into my ear. His voice was like lichen, furry and warm. And son of a gun, here he was again, Mr. Willy himself, calling in to confess his chaotic desires to me, because it was that kind of day.

"Celia, do you know who this is?" he said.

"I do know who this is," I said.

A reckless, wild feeling welled up in me. I thought about second-floor Joan making plans with her customers on the sly. All those second-floor girls seemed like heroic risk-takers to me, and I wanted to be more like them, careless and free. Something came loose in me. Something that had to do with those second-floor girls, and also, with the two knives tucked inside my new sport bag.

"I need—"

"I know what you need," I said.

"Oh?" he said.

"Don't you think we should get to know each other better, though, before I put my tight little sock on your willy?" I said.

I astounded myself, for the way I'd just talked back to this man instead of quietly putting up with his sock nonsense. He'd hang up now. I'd called his bluff. I'd never hear from him again. I could see for myself that the floor supervisor wasn't listening in on my line. He was busy dozing up there on his dais. His eyes were shut. His chest majestically rose and fell.

Mr. Willy was so quiet.

He didn't hang up.

Oh no, I thought.

"How about a little date, then, Celia?" he said. "How about tonight?"

I told him I was busy, which was true.

Mr. Willy said, "How about tomorrow at five? Would you do me the honor?"

I told him I'd never make it anywhere by five, on account of my job.

Mr. Willy said, "That's all right, Celia, I'll wait until the end of the world for you!"

"Oh, you don't need to do *that*," I said.

"How about we meet tomorrow night?" he said. "How about half past five? Will that do for you? How about we meet at half past five, in the lobby bar at the St. Francis Hotel?"

I told him I would be there. I had no intention of meeting him anywhere but at that point it felt easier to go along with his plan in a full-throated, if insincere way, than to argue with him about it.

"Oh no!" he said suddenly. "What if we miss each other in the crowd? What then?"

A childlike plaintiveness had crept into his voice. I guessed the idea of missing me in the crowd made him anxious.

"Why don't you bring along an extra sock?" I said. "Hold it where I can see it. That'll do the trick."

"Oh!" he said. "If I bring along an extra sock then you'll see me for sure!"

"For sure!" I said. "Is there anything else I can help you with today, sir?"

A little pause came. I heard it.

"I love you, Celia," Mr. Willy said.

After this declaration he hung up and for that I was grateful. The next call came in and I answered it. My day went on, same as always. The calls kept on coming. I kept on answering. Tomorrow at half past five a man with a sock in his fist would be waiting for me in the lobby bar of the St. Francis Hotel. I imagined a poor guy waving his extra sock high in the air every time the door of the place opened, to make sure his Celia saw him just as soon as she came in. What kind of sock would Mr. Willy bring? A child's sweet white sock with lace along the edge? A man's sock with a reinforced toe and heel? A silk sock? A wool one? Maybe I'd go take a peek from the door. I wouldn't go. But maybe I would. I'd peek inside. I'd spy on him from the door, the way Joan spied on her customers. I'd be totally safe. Mr. Willy didn't know what a "Celia" looked like in real life. I knew I was talking nonsense to myself and I'd never go. For one thing Drew would be counting the minutes and when I got home late there would be hell to pay. On the other hand I was always accidentally doing things that upset my Drew, so what did it matter? I could upset him without even trying. I couldn't help but wonder if it would make any difference if I went ahead one day and upset him on purpose. For the rest of the afternoon my jaw felt loose, as if someone had punched me there. I could barely speak to the customers. I could barely shape the necessary words. I felt on the edge of disintegration. When the time came for my break I went straight to the ladies' room. I took my sport bag with me. Once I'd locked myself inside the biggest stall I took the little black knife out of my bag and practiced stabbing the air many times, to work out my stress. After stabbing, I practiced slicing, experimenting with a swift backhanded gesture until it felt right to me. I kept stabbing the air, and slicing it, too, until all of my jittery feelings had calmed themselves. By then my break was over. I put my black knife back into the sport bag. I went back to my workstation, same as always. *How can I help you? How can I help you?* I said it a million times. My mind wandered once more to thoughts about the death of Vivienne Bianco. I discovered that her story had grown in my head like an especially aggressive weed, and in unexpected directions. If what Meena had said was true, then Vivienne had been strong-arming her husband for years. Maybe she'd mocked him and insulted him and told him one too many times that he was nothing but a disgusting tractor salesman who came home every night smelling of pastureland and with dirt under his nails until the day came when her endlessly coldhearted mocking cruelty had been too much for him to bear any longer and had left him with no choice but to defend himself.

I could imagine it happening that way.

Somehow it got to be five o'clock.

The floor supervisor flipped a switch. My call light went out. I was released from my headset bondage until morning. I was no longer at the mercy of those men sitting up on a dais. I could leave behind the odious paddle and go home.

As soon as I walked out the big glass doors I felt more goshawk than girl. All those hours spent tethered to a headset left me tense and waiting for the leash to yank me back. A few steps later, my body realized it could fly away freely—and then I was flying, really flying, down the sidewalk. Even though I was in that same crush of people as the day before, all of us head-down and scurrying toward the train station in a typically fruitless effort to catch the express at 5:12 instead of the local at 5:48, everything was different, because I was carrying my sport bag on one shoulder. I could hear the bright metallic sound of my dirk and my black knife clanking together inside that bag like two big metal spoons. I heard the same little song in my ear that I'd heard on the train the night before—*love and death, love and death*—and the people scurrying along the sidewalk with me, all those scurrying souls, yearning toward that train station, whipped their heads around and stared at me in wonder. Those people had heard my innermost secret thoughts. My body had shouted my secret thoughts out in every direction. All the thoughts I'd tried so hard to keep quiet. Thoughts about love and death, is what I mean. Thoughts about how love could be a land mine buried in a shimmering field of wheat, or a pistol shot, or a sticky trap set in a corner, or a noose, or an insidious addiction—and so could death be all these things. I felt wanton and loose-jointed. My body broke into a jaunty hustle. All of us rushing toward the station remembered at the same time that we were living, breathing, urgent beings who might die at any second. Just like Vivienne Bianco. Just like anyone. When we came to the station we leapt hand in hand onto the departing train. We sat closer to each other than the day before. We let our legs bump and rub as the train shook and swayed. I closed my eyes and listened to the rattle of the clackety train tracks underneath my seat.

My thoughts turned to poor Gene Bianco. The day before I'd felt pity for his poor fragile wife, poor thing, shot to death by her cold unfeeling husband for trying for her measly one chance at love with Randall Smiley. The day before I'd been certain Vivienne was the victim of a terrible act of retribution ending in death. But what if I'd got it wrong? What if Vivienne Bianco had been pushing Gene, pushing him with her bitter tart words, and her strong-arming, and her retaliatory silences whenever he displeased her, her face all twisted and ugly each night when he came home from his tractor conventions?

And I told myself Vivienne Bianco's story all over again, from this new perspective.

Here is Vivienne Bianco, the ever-superior spouse, flaunting her power over the husband, Gene Bianco, mocking him, belittling him, giving him the silent treatment, strong-arming him, telling him he's disgusting with his blue-collar interests and his tractors and his calloused workingman's hands. To rub it in she takes a lover so pitiful that it can't help but wound the pride of proud Gene Bianco. She isn't surprised by the sound of the key rattling in the lock downstairs. She has been expecting Gene all along. She is planning for her goonish husband—how in the world did she ever think she loved him?—to catch her in flagrante delicto with the feckless Randall Smiley. Oh yes, my dears. She will teach Gene Bianco a lesson he will never forget. On the day in question, Vivienne invites both men to an afternoon tryst—she invites Randall a half hour earlier, so he has plenty of time to give her his usual seven minutes of pleasure—and here comes Gene, right on time. He's coming up the slow stair, step by step, and poor Randall says: "Vivienne, it must be your husband, oh, what do we do?" And Vivienne shrugs and says, "Everything is fine, honey. Stay right where you are. It's you I love."

But Randall is no fool. He hides under the bed at the last minute. His instincts are correct. When Gene sees the incriminating evidence there on the bedroom floor, his mind snaps and his body decides to liberate itself once and for all. When I thought of Gene Bianco snapping like that my breathing grew shallow. I thought I might faint. I tried to imagine what it would be like to find myself in just that sort of hopeless, trapped situation. Then I tried to imagine what it would be like to end my suffering with a bang. I could almost imagine it.

After exhausting all possible thoughts I could think about Vivienne Bianco's bloody end, I began to think back on the way I had flown up into the air the night before, when my husband was making love to me. Up into the air I had flown, like a muscular swan, and I had hovered there above my marriage bed at an altitude where I could see things correctly. And as I'd looked down from that new vantage point, I had seen my Drew with fresh eyes. His shoulders were oily. His hands were cruel. His body was on top of me. Was that my Drew? Wasn't my Drew a good man? Wasn't Drew my savior? Hadn't my mother loved him? And here was that wily swan again, finding its way into my thoughts, and that wily old swan had just introduced to me a new thought, and the new thought was "Why don't you *do* something about it, Celia? Why don't you take that nail file out of its secret hiding place tonight and bury it in your husband's ear?" And the thought was so terrible that I tried to push it away, but try as I might I could feel it hovering there, unrepulsed, whispering its hard, true secrets, and beating its muscular wings, and not willing to be driven off altogether.

On account of my new skill of flying southward down the sidewalk toward the San Francisco station after work, I'd managed to catch the express train for once. Good thing, too, because it was a Wednesday, and every Wednesday Drew and I ate dinner at his mother's house. When I got home Drew was already standing on the front porch, waiting for me.

"What have you done to your mother's Oldsmobile?" he said.

He pointed to the cardboard I'd taped up to take the place of the broken window.

"Somebody broke into the car at the station," I said.

A wild idea came into my head, that Drew had broken that window himself.

"Did you break that window?" I said.

"Why would I break that window?" Drew said. "That's the stupidest thing I've heard you say all day."

"I'm sorry," I said.

We stood awhile. I was hoping Drew's love of punctuality would persuade him to drop this argument so we could be on our way to his mother's house.

"Anyway," Drew said. "We need to get going."

"I need to change," I said.

"You look ready enough," he said.

I didn't feel ready enough. For one thing I was carrying a sport bag with two deadly blades in it, which felt like too much firepower to bring along for dinner with my mother-in-law. Also, my blouse felt unfresh. I'd been working in it all day.

"Five minutes," Drew said.

Knowing he'd hold me to it, I ran inside. I ran to my closet and dug out a pair of boots from the back and kicked off my shoes. I pulled the boots on. I took my black knife out of my sport bag and stuck it in my left boot, pointy-end-first, in the manner the kindly cigar-smoking, mustache-wearing pawn shop guy had tutored me to wear a boot knife. It fit there like a sixth toe I'd always had and never noticed. There was a little double seam in the boot that could act as a sheath. It was as if my boot had been waiting to be introduced to my boot knife all along.

Since I could envision no need for a dirk that night, I put it away in my secret place, where I also kept my three Barbie doll heads still scarred from my childhood days, and my late mother's nail file, and the photograph of my dad, named Dirk, and the many other nostalgic and important things that I'd collected over the years. Then I took off my unfresh blouse and splashed water on my armpits and picked out a new blouse and put it on and ran back outside. Drew looked disappointed at my lack of tardiness. He hated to be wrong. We got into his car and started off. Drew's mother lived in a town called Alvarado, on the other side of the bay, across the Dumbarton Bridge from our Redwood City home. As we inched along eastward over the bridge, I looked out over the whitecapped bay, and I thought about crabs. I'd heard that all kinds of invasive species were lurking under those choppy whitecaps. I'd also heard that a species of long-legged crab had recently come to the bay, hitching a ride on Chinese barges. I could well imagine those crabs striding confidently along on the bottom of the bay and making their long-legged way up rivers and streams. One day those long-legged crabs would prevail over the weaker native species. They would conquer the wall-eyed surfperches and the anchovies and the friendly native crabs of these waters, known as "hermits." I was afraid of crabs. Not really. Not objectively. But subjectively, yes indeed. Maybe it was a residual fear I'd carried forward from the trauma of losing my mother so young. Subjectively, I knew that the Crab Queen, Bringer of Chaos and Ruler of All Beasts of Land and Air and Sea, would one day emerge from those choppy depths. On that day she would claim me as her kin. And since crabs were on my mind as we inched and struggled across the Dumbarton Bridge, I also knew that inevitably my mother-in-law would be serving fresh crab that night as a special treat, and it would turn out my guess was correct, although I ascribed no special powers of prediction to my guess, because it was peak crab season.

Drew kept talking on and on about how bad the traffic was, as if it were big news to him that rush-hour traffic was bad rather than an everyday happening. He didn't expect me to chime in with an opinion of my own and so I didn't. He was driving in his usual manner, accelerating right up to the point where he was nearly scraping the bumper of the car in front of us and then braking hard when the car in front refused to budge.

"They fired me at work," he said.

He said it so casually that I was sure I'd not heard him correctly.

"Did they fire you at work?" I said.

"What the hell, Celia," Drew said. "I just told you. They fired me at work."

"When?" I said.

"Three weeks ago," he said.

I mulled it over. Three weeks felt like a long time ago to be hearing about it just now. It wasn't the first time Drew had been fired since I'd met him, either. He kept being fired for "insubordination." I wasn't sure exactly why he was fired for insubordination so often but apparently he had a talent for it. He was running out of hospitals. Before long he'd need a brand-new career.

Somebody cut into our lane.

Drew honked and hit the brakes and then we lurched forward.

"Fucking doctors," Drew said. "They think they know better. Fucking, fucking doctors."

"Why did they fire you this time?" I said. "Was it for insubordination again?"

"This is why I don't tell you things," Drew said. "You always make it out to be like it's my fault."

I pondered awhile.

"So what's your plan?" I said.

"Jesus, Celia, is that all you can say? Why can't you support me for once?"

"Fucking doctors," I said. "I can't believe those fucking doctors fired you again."

The knotty tension in Drew's face relaxed.

"Fucking doctors," he agreed.

FIVE

KEEP MOVING THROUGH IT

Drew's mother's name was Augusta Dent and she was a widow. She had a stern demeanor. Drew always insisted vociferously that his mother was a crack-up and the life of every party but I had yet to see these qualities in her myself. She lived in the same house in Alvarado where she and her husband, an avid hunter, had raised their only son. That town was famous for its Spanish-era cemetery, a place where monks and Indigenous peoples were buried side by side. Drew always knocked on his mother's door as if he hadn't grown up in that house to begin with. His mother always opened the door and invited us in as if we were sketchy guests rather than familiar family. She always kissed me lightly on one cheek and sprang away as if she thought I might bite her. She called her son daily to check on whether I was treating him right. I could hear her voice through the telephone wires whenever Drew picked up the line. Her unwavering dislike of me seeped from the receiver and stuck to the walls of our home like black mold no matter how diligently I tried to scrub it off.

"Hello, Mother," Drew said.

"You look thin, son," Augusta said.

Augusta led us into her parlor, the way she always did. I always thought of the word *parlor* for that room. I could never think of Augusta's parlor as a "living room" or a "den" or a "sitting room." Maybe I felt this way because the town was old, and this house was old, and naturally, this room was an old sort of room, one that deserved an old-fashioned name like "parlor." It was the kind of room where funerals and wakes and séances were probably held back in the day. Augusta's parlor was stuffed full of furniture. The walls were covered with dead animal parts, nailed up. Skins. Antlers. Horns. Heads of beasts that stared out into space with terrified glass eyes. A wild boar's tusky bust hung above the door to the kitchen—one tusk sawed off, apparently by Drew when he was a boy and wanted to take that tooth along with him to school to show his friends. The boar seemed upset about the missing tusk. It glared down at me with its small glass eyes as if I'd violated that tusk myself.

A trophy-of-trophies hung above the mantel. A stag of some kind, its neck still straining with bulgy muscles as if that deer were about to leap away from the hunter's bullet. Too late, my hooved friend. The bullet got you. There must have been a master taxidermist somewhere in the picture to have made that deer's straining neck muscles look so alive, and that deer had a rack of antlers so huge that its points stuck out into space.

I'd heard many a tale of Drew's hunting adventures with his late father. One of the adjustments I'd needed to make after Drew moved in with me was to get used to living with his guns, along with the enormous gun safe he'd brought with him. That safe took up half the space in the second bedroom. Drew's love of the hunt clarified for me what drove his fierce understandings of right and wrong, and up and down, and winners and losers. He'd killed his first big buck when he was eleven. He still carried on with the sport, following in the footsteps of his beloved father, and following the seasons, disappearing for days or weeks into the manly wilderness and returning to fill our big freezer with venison and elk, and boar and bear. In case you're wondering, bear meat tastes like berries and acorns, and it leaves an aftertaste of honey in the mouth. I kid you not. More proof, in my opinion, that "you are what you eat."

"Sit," Augusta said, and we sat.

Drew sat next to me. Augusta sat across from us. Drew draped his arm over my shoulders. His loving gesture bent me forward at the neck until my head felt disconnected from the rest of my body. My glass-eyed gaze was directed downward, toward the coffee table in front of us. The finish on the table was stained with concentric circles where damp champagne flutes and coffee cups had rested over the years. The magazines were from the sixties. I began to tap my foot, partly from nervousness, and partly to remind myself of the little black knife inside my boot. Reminding myself about the knife in my boot led me to remind myself that I didn't in fact need to submit to Drew's heavy arm pressing against my neck, and in one deft neck-gesture I released myself and sat free of him and his heavy arm.

"What the heck is the matter with you?" Drew said.

"Your wife is in one of her moods again, I see," Augusta said.

I could smell the crabs baking in the kitchen beyond. Stuffed crab in the shell, no doubt. Augusta made her famous stuffed crab dish every year in the fresh-crab season. She spooned the meat out of its shell, mixed it up with mysterious ingredients, stuffed it back into its shell, and baked it. She served the crabs with their eyes still attached. There were small shreds of crabmeat still clinging to her hands.

"Stuffed crab, tonight?" Drew said.

Augusta nodded, a little grimly.

"I know how much you love it, son," she said. "It's a lot of work. Sometimes a lot of work is the only way to get what you want in life."

"Celia would tell you the work isn't worth it," Drew said. "She doesn't like crabs. She's afraid of crabs."

Drew and Augusta looked at me with what they probably thought was a friendly silent look. They were inviting me to join in the conversation, and to explain my fear of crabs to them. I silently declined their invitation. In the pause that followed, Drew interjected more information about me into the conversation on my behalf.

"Celia believes in the Crab Queen," he said.

This wasn't a true fact about me. The truth was this. When I was eight or nine, I'd seen an old movie on TV called *Attack of the Killer Crab Queen*. The hero in that movie is a female crab as big as a six-story building and her sole purpose in life is to carry off scantily clad women in her claws. She mesmerizes the captive women with her glowing stalks of eyes. Slowly she builds an Army of Woman, legions of women, whose sole purpose is to destroy the rational world of Man and replace it with chaotic female energy.

I didn't believe in the Crab Queen. Of course not. Sometimes I thought about the Crab Queen, that's all. Sometimes I allowed happy superstitions into my way of thinking, as a way to cope. It was a coping tradition my mother had passed on to me. My mother taught me that not all that is true in this world is comprehensible to our tiny human minds. She also taught me that there is no harm in entertaining happy superstitions. Entertaining happy superstitions isn't the same thing as believing in things. It's more on the level of knocking on wood, or saying "Bless you" when somebody sneezes. Drew and Augusta were both looking at me expectantly, and maybe derisively. They were still waiting for me to explain my droll thoughts about the Crab Queen, so they could share a good laugh. Instead, I said a silent prayer to the Crab Queen. I asked her to deliver me from a conversation that seemed tailor-made to mock me. And maybe the Crab Queen heard me, because Drew and Augusta suddenly changed the subject of their conversation and began to chat back and forth energetically about their mutual love of *Jonathan Livingston Seagull*, a surprise bestseller in those times. Augusta loved it for the pictures. Drew loved it for its deeper meanings. They didn't ask my opinion. I was free to think my own thoughts. I could have thought about my day at work, I suppose, or about my burgeoning interest in true-crime stories, or about so many other topics that interested me, but my mind landed on a memory from my childhood days, and since at some point I will need to divulge the details of what I did when I was eleven years old that led my mother to conclude I was destined to follow in the nefarious footsteps of my father, the bounder, it might as well be now.

It happened after I met my friend. My lovely friend. Her name was Joe, and the thing is, I loved her. Eleven is an age when notions about bodies and their parts are vague and inconsequential. Eleven is an age when girls are banished to a frigid existence, no longer welcome on laps or into the bath at bathtime. Eleven is an age when bodies become prisons of wretched isolation. Inside my body the earth trembled and shook. Outside my body I was banished to a cold place. Then here comes this girl. This love. She moves in across the street. A day comes when clothes feel like wretched unnecessary barriers to our closeness, and we take them off, not shyly—there is no shame in those girls—but patiently, and with serious purpose. Neither one of those girls is laughing. They are committed to what happens next. One girl lies on top of her friend. Now that the unnecessary clothing is no longer in the way, she feels the breasts of the other girl pushing into her like hard little raisins. She likes the way those little raisins push themselves into her flatness. She is three months older but her body has yet to change in any way, and so the feel of her friend's little breasts, against her plank of a chest, fills her with sweet anticipation. Heat comes like a beating pulse. There is an egg in one girl's throat because the other girl is sucking on her lower lip. "Oh," one of them says, and lifts her chin, exposing a long pale neck to kiss. The two of them rub and shudder. They push and turn. The world grows so quiet, so small. Before long the whole world equals just those girls. Their bodies take up all the space in the world and then some. Together they stumble onto the knowledge of how good it feels to rub each other between their legs. It feels so good that they keep doing it until they go blind and deaf. They can't hear the mother calling up the stairs that lunch is ready. The mother comes up to investigate. She opens the door and hollers and pulls the neighbor-girl up by the hair and slaps her twice across the face—*slap, slap*—and covers her own naked, crying kid with a bedspread. Then she strong-arms the slutty-wise other girl down the stairs and straight out of the house and slams the door behind her without giving that girl a chance to retrieve her clothes. The mother sinks to her knees and keens back and forth. She stays there, keening, by the door, until her husband comes home. After the husband hears the whole goddamn perverted story from his wife, he calls the police. The other girl is three months older and she looks like a boy. Clearly that other girl, the one called Celia, is criminally delinquent, or maybe insane. Celia's mother loves harmony even more than she loves to sew and so she takes the neighbors' side. She isn't about to defend her daughter when the whole neighborhood has turned against that odd flat-chested girl. She begins to second-guess her girl's every step and word. For years she sends her girl to summer Bible camp in an effort to cure the girl's suspicious proclivities. The mother tries to teach the girl about the needle, about sewing, about stitching things up good and tight. She can't for the life of her understand how clumsy and uninterested the girl is these days when she used to love all fabric arts. Now that girl can't sit still. It's because that girl has been distracted by the glory of touching and being touched. She can't keep from thinking all the time how her skin is touching-tasting and touching-breathing, how good it feels to be alive in this skin! When she sees animals coupling—bugs, dogs, pigeons in the park—her body trembles and she wants to see her friend.

In the meantime the friendship between those two girls is busily being erased from human history until it's as if those two girls never touched at all. Here is Celia playing alone in her yard, throwing a ball against the garage door and catching it. Here is Joe, emerging diaphanously from the house across the street. Joe is dressed in a fancy dress and on her way to "Junior Cotillion." Joe's entire wardrobe has changed to soft pink tulle overnight.

As for Celia, she wears T-shirts. She begins to chew on her tongue. Eventually her natural talent for giving and receiving body-joy is so resoundingly crushed by circumstance that she forgets all about it. Her body is a dead shell of a body and she barely remembers those giddy child-feelings she once knew.

Years pass and crumble to dust. The mother still hasn't forgotten the *event*. Not a day goes by without the mother thinking about it. The weight of all that worry about her daughter's randy ways causes the mother's body to turn on itself, and then, she dies. Before she dies, though, the mother thinks it's only fair to tell the girl's new boyfriend about the girl's perverted, promiscuous past. That man should know the truth before he settles on Celia in a meaningful way. The man's knowledge of the *event* reinforces his abiding conviction that the girl, now his wife, will need his constant guidance and correction, and he will cherish her, and honor her, and keep her in line, and let her know who is boss, as long as they both shall live.

And now we have arrived at a critical turning point in this story, when a doomed stuffed crab looks up at Celia from Augusta's fine-bone-china dinner plate.

That crab catches Celia's eye at last.

Watch out, Celia, the doomed crab whispers, *or one day they'll scoop out your innards and bake them and stuff them back in again.*

"Tell me more about *sterile fields,* son," Augusta is saying.

Augusta can never hear enough about her son's life as a scrub tech.

On our way home from Wednesday dinners with Augusta, Drew liked to stop at the local indoor shooting range. The range was less than a mile away from his childhood home. For Drew, shooting guns was like exercising a prize horse. You needed to do it regularly, or the gun, or horse, would feel neglected. Soon the gun or horse would grow flaccid and irritable and it wouldn't do what you wanted it to. Before we'd left home he'd filled the trunk of his car with many pistols, which he now brought out and took with him into the gun range. I felt ludicrous following my well-armed husband into the range with my secret boot knife. What did a boot knife matter? What could a boot knife do, if it ever came to that? Nothing. Nothing at all.

When we were first dating, Drew had gifted me a little .38 Special, a gun that fit easily into my small hands and had barely any recoil. He had chosen that coy gun for me back when he'd still held out hope that I would one day join him in the sport he so loved. But after the first few sessions I would not be persuaded to take up my .38 Special from its case. Over time that little gun had become Drew's gun by proxy. And so he was surprised when I asked to shoot it myself that night. I needed to borrow ear protection. I chose a lane far away from my husband. I shot a few rounds. I wanted to see if I liked guns any better than before, but I did not. It didn't move me in any way to shoot bullets from that .38 Special. Guns had always seemed mechanical and emotionless to me when compared with the alternatives. I shot poorly, and before long Drew came over, to teach me a lesson. He put his arms around me. Drew enjoyed teaching me lessons, of many kinds. He was practically squeezing the trigger himself.

"Get off me," I said.

There must have been something untoward about my body language, because all the men in the range, who moments ago had been entirely absorbed with shooting off their pistols and revolvers, stopped shooting and looked my way, as if they were trying to assess a new threat in their midst.

The big guy who managed the place came over.

"How's tricks?" he said.

"My wife isn't feeling well," Drew said. "She's in a mood."

The two men looked at me serenely until I surrendered my .38 Special to my husband. I walked out of the soundproofed range and into a room by the entrance where the wives had gathered to wait for their men to finish shooting off their pistols. Those wives were knitters. It was an art my mother had tried and failed to teach me. Some of the wives had brought cute little fluffy dogs along. Those dogs were curled up at their mistresses' feet. Since I had no dog, and since I was not a knitter, both dogs and knitters looked at me askance. I sat by myself until closing time, when Drew came to collect me.

On the way home I could tell by the way Drew was breathing in shallow sniffs and snorts that he and I were heading straight for a tussle. We were all the way back across the Dumbarton Bridge before he spoke up.

"I don't know why you're like this," he said.

"Like what?"

He smiled. The way he did sometimes.

"You know what I'm talking about," he said. "I'm talking about how you manage to be as unpleasant as possible at all times. Here's my mother, trying so hard to be like a mother to you. She treats you like the daughter she never had. The way you act toward her makes me sick. You act like a three-year-old child when we visit her. You have tantrums over every small thing. You need to make yourself the center of attention. Why did you push me away when I wanted to put my arm around you? Do you know how that makes me feel? Why are you always turning your nose up at my mother's cooking? What the hell happened at the gun range?"

"I don't like the taste of crab," I said.

"Such a baby," Drew said. "Now you're going to cry."

But I didn't cry. Why wasn't I crying? I wondered about it. I didn't want to argue with Drew—and yet, I *did* want to argue with him. I didn't want to stoke his angry feelings—and yet, I didn't care about his angry feelings. I knew it was a good idea to apologize—and yet, I never wanted to apologize to him again. It was the fault of that little black knife in my boot. The little black knife changed everything. With a black knife in my boot, I could speak with Drew man-to-man. And because of that black knife—because I'd bought that small, clever concealed little weapon of my very own—it seemed likely that my husband and I were about to enter a wild untrodden territory together when it came to how we settled our differences. To mark this change in our marital relationship I turned on the radio. Drew turned it off. I turned it back on. Drew decided to raise the stakes and took the next turn too sharply and ran the car up over a curb, and then we were heading straight into a big tree, and that would be the end of my small rebellion, because he and I were about to be dead, but at the last second Drew swerved and instead of ramming us both head-on into a tree he just rammed us into a tree on my side. When the car hit that tree all the air left my body. Probably my soul left my body, too. Then my soul decided to come back. I didn't die. By this time the car was at a standstill. A little tilted. All was not well. Drew and I sat there, motionless. I listened to the engine ping and sigh. Somehow a bunch of twigs and leaves had forced their way in through my closed window and my lap was full of tree parts. My body was a clenched fist. I was breathing in small gasping desperate teaspoonfuls of air that left me feeling starved for oxygen and close to suffocation.

"What the hell, Celia," Drew said.

"I'm hurt," I said.

It was a reflexive comment. I wasn't sure yet if I was hurt. I'd just been in an accident. It was too soon for me to gauge how bad the accident had been. Stabs of pain were running up and down my spine and I was still trying to decide if the stabs were significant. I was beginning to wonder whether I'd cracked a rib or two. Possibly I was suffering from a punctured lung, or internal bleeding.

"You're all right," Drew said.

He took a deep breath and blew it out.

"I'm all right, too," he said. "Thanks for asking."

He got out of the car and began to look it over for damage. I could see for myself that the windshield was cracked and the hood was crumpled. Drew was examining the front fender on my side. He leaned down and glared at what he saw. The headlights were still working and they lit Drew's face up from below and made him look unusually demonic. Then he ran a finger along my side of the car, and I heard him say: "Three hundred dollars at least."

He walked all around the car, bending and peering, before he got back in.

"I think she'll still drive," he said.

"Then drive me to a hospital," I said.

"Aren't you all right?" Drew said.

I told him my ribs hurt and I was having trouble breathing. He turned on the dome light and looked at me skeptically. I wanted him to be frantic with worry for my well-being. I wanted him to apologize for ramming me into a tree. These desires seemed too obvious to mention and it depressed me that my husband didn't know the first thing about how to behave after a car accident.

"I want to go home," I said. "Let's just go home."

"Right," he said.

Drew began to drive. Whenever he turned the wheel to the right, the car made a grating sound of metal scraping against metal. We got home, though. All I wanted was to be inside my own house. Drew was preoccupied with the damage done to the car and had no time for me and so I made the long lonely journey to the front door by myself. Each step made my stabs of pain stab all the more stabbingly, until I began to wonder whether a rib in my chest had come loose and was about to skewer an important organ. I was moving with glacial slowness. I could hear Drew, behind me, somewhere, swearing at the car. I made it to the front door and opened it and slumped into my mother's favorite armchair. After a while Drew brought me a glass of water and two codeine tablets left over from the time when he'd had oral surgery.

"You'll be all right," he said. "Keep moving through it."

Drew had been a big athlete in high school. He had lettered in track. His specialty had been the high jump, an event in which his lithe coiled body had given him an advantage over other boys. Sometimes when he gave me advice, I could hear echoes of his former coaches.

"And you need to stop *tensing*," he said. "It's never as bad as it feels. You need to keep moving through it!"

"Okay," I said.

I grunted a time or two while Drew stood there looking at my huddled pathetic self. He was probably thinking that these antics of mine—the way I slumped there, breathing in shallow bursts through tightly clenched teeth—was a manipulative con. He probably thought I was pretending to be hurt as a way to win the argument. I began to cry. Drew was probably thinking I was just pretending to cry to garner his undeserved sympathy. Maybe Drew was right. Maybe I wasn't hurt. I just needed to keep moving through it. Maybe these were crocodile tears. Maybe it was my fault.

"I'm sorry," I said.

"You shouldn't have started in on me like that," Drew said.

SIX

THE SOCK MAN

In the morning I'd wonder if my possibly cracked ribs had saved me from some feisty corrective holding from my husband the night before. It could be that Drew had looked me over and decided I'd been taught enough of a lesson already. He went straight to sleep. But I couldn't sleep. I was up all night, trying and failing to get comfortable. I watched TV until the channels signed off with the national anthem and left me with nothing to watch but TV snow. When it got to be close enough to dawn for me to stop pretending I would fall asleep eventually, I splashed water on my face and dressed for work. I kept trying to move through it but my face kept twisting itself into a gaping yawn of pain. I caught a glimpse of my gaping yawn in the bathroom mirror before I left for work and the expression on my face seemed exaggerated even to me. No wonder Drew discounted my complaints.

When I came back into the bedroom for my keys, Drew's eyes were open and he was looking straight at me.

"I love you," he whispered.

I was a little bit afraid of him. I decided it would be best if I kissed him good-bye. I made sure to kiss him in the way he liked to be kissed by me—that is, the opposite of moistly. He looked at me lovingly. Or at least it was one of those looks that I'd always interpreted as "love" in the past. Lately I wasn't so sure what those looks might have meant.

A few minutes later I found myself driving along my usual

route to the train station, where I caught the first train to come along. My body kept contemplating its encounter with a big tan oak the night before. I had more trouble than usual listening to the voices in the train car that morning. The words were full of interference, like a radio signal coming through heavy static.

That's what his trumpet teacher said.

old family recipe

black blake stab slice brick slip

I must have dozed off about then, because by the time the train reached the city I was so fast asleep that the conductor needed to shake my shoulder.

"Ow," I said.

"Fourth and Townsend, end of the line," the conductor said. "Rough night, lady?"

I didn't appreciate the insinuations embedded in his comment about my rough night. I didn't answer. Not that he expected an answer. He'd moved on. I got myself off the train and hobbled straight down Fourth Street to the office where I took the elevator up to the cafeteria. I kept moving through it. After I picked out my jelly doughnut and poured a coffee and paid for them I saw Helen sitting alone at a table by the window. When she saw me she stood up and shouted, "Jesus Christ, Celia, what *happened* to you?" and pulled a chair out and guided me into it.

"Car accident," I said grittily.

"Holy shit. Why are you at work?" Helen said.

Helen's salty language invigorated me. She pulled her chair close to mine and began to rub me in unlikely places, on my cheeks, on the top of my head.

"It's not that bad," I said. "I just need to keep moving through it."

"Shit," Helen said. "You sound like my acupuncturist."

"No, I mean it," I said. "It's never as bad as it feels."

"That's crazy-talk," Helen said. "How can it not be as bad as it feels? It's exactly as bad as it feels. How bad you *feel* equals how bad things *are*. Right?"

I felt magically better. It was as if Helen's random vigorous rubs and salty opinions had set my ribs back into place. When she was done with the rubbing, we sat together silently for some minutes, chewing and staring into space, and then out of the blue Helen said to me: "Do you ever hear voices even when you're not plugged in?" It was one of those times that come along in life when somebody's offhand comment makes you feel entirely understood. I wanted to leap up and yodel. Instead, I nodded, and Helen smiled off into the distance, as if to say: "Well, what do you know, Celia. Maybe you and I are not as peculiar as we supposed ourselves to be, because I, like you, hear voices even when I'm not plugged in."

"What do your voices say to you?" Helen said.

"They tell me I'd better watch out, mostly," I said. "Because the world is a chaotic place. People like me need to be ready for anything."

"People like *us*, you mean," Helen said.

"Yes," I said. "People like us."

Helen squeezed my hand and let go. My soul breathed in and out. Then the fragile closeness we were beginning to share, back and forth, was shattered when Meena and Joan and Tammy all showed up at once at our table and sat down, and the sounds in the cafeteria grew high-spirited and edgy, and the sunlight pouring through the window grew more intense, and Helen's face changed, from an open and unguarded face to a wise and cynical face. I watched it happen.

"What's the news from the third floor, Celia?" Joan said.

Joan's question was like a cattle prod to my brain. I felt compelled to share my news about Mr. Willy and the date I had made with him at the lobby bar in the St. Francis Hotel that night, and that, instead of a red carnation, I'd asked Mr. Willy to bring a sock and to hold it prominently in his hand, so I could find him in the crowd, because that man was always talking about socks. He was obsessed with them.

"Hey, I know that guy!" Joan said. "I used to be his favorite! He used to call me every day! Now he's found Celia. You sly devil, Celia! He threw me over for a younger woman, and that woman was you!"

"I remember that guy," Meena said. "I remember his kind voice, and his interest in talking to me about the wicking properties of socks."

"I used to call him the Sock Man," Joan said. "You're a sly one, Celia! Making a secret rendezvous behind my back with my Sock Man!"

"It's not like I'm planning to go," I said.

"You should go," Meena said. "You should go take a good look at him and then come back and report to us what you learn about him."

"We should all go," Joan said. "I always wanted to see for myself what the Sock Man had up his sleeve—"

"Or in his sock," Tammy said.

"I can't," I said. "My husband doesn't like it when I come home late."

"Jesus, Mary, and Joseph," Joan said. "Your husband is not the boss of you. You have every right to go out with us whenever you feel like it."

"You take the train, right?" Meena said. "We can drink one round and then you can take a taxi to the station. I promise, honey. I'll get you home in time to satisfy your precious husband. You'll be home before he knows it. Just one round."

"I can't," I said.

My voice sounded unexpectedly whiny and resentful. This change in tone made me wonder if I was considering going out with those second-floor girls to spy on Mr. Willy, the Sock Man. Maybe it was just my body that was considering it, though, and not my mind. To my mind, the idea of going out with those girls for winks and drinks still felt wild and fanciful. I had never come home later than the local at 5:48 would get me there, and even then it seemed too late for Drew. I wasn't sure what the consequences would be if I ever got home later than that.

Just then I thought back on the way my husband had steered me into a big tan oak the night before. Maybe the memory of a big tree rushing toward me should have given me pause, and made me cautious, but instead the memory left me feeling cantankerous and contrarian and defiant, and I told myself that Drew wasn't the boss of me. Not in the least. Never had been.

"Okay, let's do it," I said.

By the time we left the cafeteria to get to our workstations I felt like a brand-new girl, buoyed up by the idea that Drew was not the boss of me.

Then I heard a little voice, whispering, next to my right ear.

I'm afraid, said the little voice.

"What are you afraid of, little voice?" I asked it.

I'm afraid of Drew, the little voice said.

That voice sounded so much like my own voice, though, that I didn't trust it.

Instead, I banished it.

"Go away," I said.

Away it flew.

Drew called in at about nine that morning. He identified himself this time. He had called in to the floor supervisor's line so he'd be connected to me straightaway. The supervisor gave me the heads-up and said to keep the conversation snappy because the call queue wasn't getting any shorter. Then he transferred Drew's call over to my workstation.

"My car is shot," Drew said. "It's not worth trying to salvage."

"What?" I said.

Drew told me his car wouldn't start because the battery had, it turned out, been imperceptibly cracked in the accident the night before. All night long, that battery had been dripping acid over important engine parts. The car had been secretly dissolving itself all night. Drew discovered these facts about his car only after I'd made my early getaway. I was already at work, and I was glad, because it seemed likely that my righteously indignant husband was about to tell me his car was ruined on account of me. It was probably better that I was here at the office and not standing right in front of him when he told me it was all my fault.

"God damn it, Celia," Drew said.

"I'm sorry," I said.

"It never would have happened if you hadn't started that pig-headed argument with me about the radio," he said.

I accepted it. The accident was all my fault. If I hadn't turned on the radio a second time then Drew wouldn't have taken the next turn too sharply. If he hadn't taken the turn too sharply, then Drew wouldn't have driven up over that curb. And so on and so on all the way back to Adam and Eve and everyone knew that what happened between those two original humans was all Eve's fault. It all tracked. Drew had trained me so well in this subtle and sophisticated way of thinking that any other interpretation of past events seemed highly implausible and almost unthinkable even in my wildest imaginings. It was impossible for me to think about his ruined car in any other light than this: that I had done the ruining.

"I need to buy a new car, thanks to you," he said. "And you are going to pay for it."

He said it matter-of-factly. He sounded reasonable. The way he always did. Then I reminded myself of the new way of thinking those second-floor girls had introduced me to.

"Maybe you shouldn't have driven your car into a tree," I said. "Seems to me you were the one who did that. Not me."

"What the hell is wrong with you?" Drew said.

"I'm going out with friends tonight," I said. "I'll be home a little late."

"Don't push me, Celia," Drew said.

"Gotta go," I said. I ended the call.

I can't believe I did that. I still get a cold rush of feeling running down my spine when I think of the way I hung up on my husband rather than listen to what he had to say to me. Most of the time I tried to listen to the voices in my ear without hanging up or banishing them impetuously before they'd had their full say. It was my job to listen. I always did my best to treat each voice with the tender care it deserved. Then again, some voices aren't helpful. They need to be banished. There was always a danger, though, of making a mistake about which voices to listen to and which to banish. Sometimes it was hard for me to pick out the true signal from the random noise. It didn't help that the floor supervisors had the radio blaring up on their dais all day. The supervisors were mostly in their fifth decade of life and they liked to listen to a local station that rebroadcast Gene Autry's *Melody Ranch* radio show from days gone by. *I'm back in the saddle again. I'm a Yankee Doodle Dandy.* Beyond the little voice I'd heard at the beginning of the workday, and Drew's call, and Gene Autry's sad laments, I can't remember any of the other voices that flowed into my ear although there must have been plenty of them. I took care of people's problems by instinct. My mind was too full of a brand-new thought to pay much attention to what customers said to me. The brand-new glorious drumbeat of a thought was: "Drew is not the boss of me." Those second-floor girls had stirred up a radical notion in my brain that maybe I was my own boss. I could do whatever I wanted to do and be whatever I wanted to be. I could be a wandering restless urge. I could be a muscular swan, or a goshawk, or a member of an elite fighting force, or a ragged crab scuttling across the floor of ancient seas—and for one night I was going to be a third-floor girl, going out for winks and drinks with her second-floor pals.

At five o'clock I ripped the headset off and hung it up on its hook and took the elevator down to wait for the second-floor girls to gather. Here was a fine surprise: Randall Smiley was standing there in the lobby. Maybe the Mob was no longer after him because he looked as relaxed as pecan pie on a Sunday afternoon. When the next elevator arrived its doors opened and Meena came sashaying out and walked over and kissed Randall on the cheek while he stood there importantly. Randall must have felt like a returning war hero because people kept stopping to say hello. They wanted to shake his hand. Even though he'd been fired and disgraced, and had broken a commandment or two, and had blood on his hands in the opinion of some, he was still our latest celebrity. Helen came gliding out of the next elevator to come along and she walked over and handed me some foil packets and a Dixie cup with water in it and said: "Valium, for the pain." I thought it was kind of her, and I said so. Once Tammy and Joan came to join us we began to walk in the direction of the St. Francis Hotel. It wasn't just Tammy and Meena and Helen and Joan and me and Randall walking along, either. There was a crowd of us phone company workers by then, with Randall leading us. I couldn't tell which of the phone company employees in that crowd were coming along to spy on the Sock Man, and which of them hadn't heard the first thing about the Sock Man plan and were tagging along for no other reason than they were excited to be going out with a celebrity of Randall Smiley's caliber. As I strode along with all those phone company folks I felt as if I were going to a party, or a wedding, or a protest march. Our voices sounded like a chorus of raucous jubilant voices. Randall Smiley kept adding his big hearty bass laughs to the mix.

"What does Randall Smiley have to laugh about?" Helen said.

Helen was walking along next to me. I'd just noticed her there.

"It's like he forgets he was part of a blood-soaked tragedy not so long ago," Helen said.

"I've heard that learning to laugh again is an important part of the healing process," I said.

The healing process was all the rage that year. I'd read about it in the magazines. People were willy-nilly joining retreats in the woods where they would be ritualistically humiliated and not allowed to go to the bathroom until they learned to walk over beds of coals without burning the soles of their feet.

"I guess so," Helen said. "Yeah."

I decided I liked Helen. A lot. I liked the way her personality was a mix of perspicacity and fantastical conspiratorial thinking. It is a combo you don't often come across in daily life, and it resembled my own internal landscape to a T. She was beginning to fade at the edges. All of them were. Valium was a new substance to my body and I could feel it wrapping itself around my troubles like an Ace bandage.

When we got to the hotel a doorman greeted us. He was wearing a red suit with a bib for a collar, and red tights. Later I learned that his getup was fashioned after a traditional uniform worn by the Yeoman Warders of the Tower of London, which might explain why the man looked preposterous out here in front of a hotel on Union Square in San Francisco—but who am I to judge? This doorman looked tranquil, and I admired him for that. He had learned how to transport himself to another place while performing his menial duties with exactitude. Allowing oneself to fly freely away from tedious work is an important skill for the working class. It saves us from alcoholism and early death.

We phone company folk were a rowdy bunch compared with the rest of the crowd inside the St. Francis Hotel. Most people in the bar were quietly going about their business. They were drinking sophisticated drinks, like scotch on the rocks—nothing fancy or colorful, or garnished with a paper parasol—and they were chatting in low undertones. They were soberly holding their liquor. By comparison, we phone company folk already sounded drunk.

Randall hailed a waiter or two and directed them to push some tables together for our awkwardly large party. After the tables were pushed into one long table, we arrived at that uncomfortable time that always comes along just before people in a big group begin to jockey for position and sit down. No one wants to sit off in a corner with people they don't like. No one wants to look pushy by sitting down first, in the middle. Thank goodness for Randall Smiley. He had no such thoughts in his head. He chose a seat for himself in the middle and sat himself down like a visiting dignitary.

Randall Smiley had become the undisputed focal point for our party by then. Meena sat down next to him. She might have vaguely remembered the original purpose of our gathering because she said, "Come on over here, Celia! Sit next to me!" and patted the empty chair to her right, but Joan got there first. I was in an awful panic by this time because there was a man sitting at the bar who was holding a prominent sock in his hand. I sat down in one of those dreaded corner seats, with my back to the bar. I didn't trust myself to sit any other way. I would have kept looking at the man with the sock if I had. The Sock Man would find me out by my stares. Instead, I sat surreptitiously.

Randall ordered two pitchers of frozen margaritas and two pitchers of beer.

"Fried calamari all around," he added.

Helen sat down next to me, at the skinny end of our long, long table.

"Jesus Christ, Celia, there's a man sitting at the bar with a sock in his hand," Helen said.

"I know," I said. "I can't look."

"I'll look for you," Helen said. "He's about forty-seven, I'd say. Comb-over. He's wearing a suit and tie. It looks like he dolled up for you, honey."

A pitcher of margaritas came my way and I poured myself some, and so did Helen. I was breaking the law twice over by then. First by being an underage drinker, but no one seemed to mind in the least. Second by concealing my boot knife, which no one knew about but me. I dazzled myself with my two-times-daring. My drink tasted like snow. It seemed a frivolous drink to me. A child's drink. There are many rules I have come to discover about how much and how fast to drink when out with work friends but at the time I was still ignorant of those rules. I drank too fast. My faux pas caught Randall's attention.

"Celia's thirsty, pour her another one," Randall said commandingly.

The pitcher came around again.

"Holy cow, Celia, there's a man sitting at the bar with a sock in his hand!" Meena said, in less than a whisper.

"Oh," Helen said. "The Sock Man is coming this way."

I could feel the Sock Man coming closer even though my back was to him. The coming of the Sock Man felt like a slow river of hot lava oozing in my direction. I felt him standing behind me. I felt his eyes scraping over all our faces, one by one, or in my case I felt his eyes scraping over the back of my head.

"Celia?" said a voice, just behind me.

"That's me!" Joan said. "I'm Celia!"

It was a Spartacus moment if there ever was one. I could feel the Sock Man standing behind me with a sock in his hand. He'd be wondering what to do next. He'd imagined a cozy tête-à-tête with his favorite phone company gal. Not this rowdy crowd. No one invited him to pull up a chair. The woman who had identified herself as "Celia" was flanked by good pals on both sides and she didn't seem inclined to join him in a dark romantic corner.

As for Joan, she had never looked so much like a Joan to me. Whereas my Celia-ness was screaming out of my body in every direction. I was certain the Sock Man could sense me, the real me, sitting so close that he could have reached out and tapped me on the head if he'd wanted to, in a "duck, duck, goose" sort of way.

Joan was staring back at the Sock Man with flirty defiance and then she smirked a small smirk. It must have dawned on the Sock Man about then that he was being made a fool of and that his Celia was the cause of this public embarrassment. Nobody could move on from this tense situation. We'd come to a time in our lives that was a perfectly balanced impasse between equal and opposite forces. On the one side was Mr. Willy's desire to connect with his Celia. On the other side was Joan's desire to ridicule him for it. I was just a spectator.

"You're not Celia," Mr. Willy slowly said. "Your look is all wrong."

"That's a fine thing to say to a lady," Joan said.

The Sock Man stood his ground. He did not slink away. I could feel him trying to locate the true Celia in that throng of phone company employees. The hairs at the nape of my neck sensed a man of unusual propensities, standing inches away. Why had I allowed the Sock Man to be ridiculed this way? I, too, had unusual propensities. I, too, had been the object of ridicule and scorn throughout my life. I, too, had filled my daydreams with gentle sexual perversions, and some not so gentle perversions. Later in life I would think long and hard about the ways we humans impose our narrow definitions of acceptable behavior on each other, and the way we're taught as children to never speak of socks, or long-legged crabs for that matter, out of context. That's when I felt the slightest whisper of a touch, there, on my right shoulder. I didn't move my head. Just my eyes. What I saw was a sock. Draped there on my shoulder, by a well-manicured hand. The hand was patting the sock into place. And as I stared down at that sock, that hand, the mysterious happenings in my recent past came together in a jolt, and I knew myself. I'd felt the first small stirrings of revelatory insight after the death of Vivienne Bianco. Then a black knife had come to me. Then a stuffed crab had looked up at me from Augusta's dinner plate with recognition in its eyes. Now this Sock Man had dubbed me with his sock, and had claimed me as kin, and I remembered what I had always known: I was Daughter of Dirk. I was Minion of the Crab Queen. I was in a full fever. I wasn't a normal girl. I was supernatural. I was uncanny. I was magnificent.

"Look, bub, we don't want you here," Randall said.

He snapped his fingers at a passing red jacket.

"Waiter! Garçon! This queer man is harassing us!"

The man in the red jacket came over.

The Sock Man's hand retreated from my shoulder.

The sock remained.

"Waiter. This man is bothering the ladies," Randall said.

"Sir, you're going to have to leave the premises," the waiter said.

"I get it," the Sock Man said. "You think I don't belong here. You think I'm the troublemaker in this situation, and not these good people. But you're wrong."

"I don't think you're the troublemaker in this situation," the waiter said. "I don't think anything. These good people want you to move away from their table. Please go."

I felt the Sock Man's chaotic energy surge up, and then, recede.

"He's leaving," Helen said.

"He's gone," Helen said.

A full pitcher of frozen margaritas came by and Helen poured me another one. I took a long drink. I set my glass down. Now that the Sock Man had gone away—now that his chaotic, nearly radioactive energies were no longer close enough to excite my nape hairs, or to spark revelatory insight into my true nature—I felt less sure of myself. Already I was second-guessing my recent revelations. Instead of marveling in my specialness I began to remind myself that I was an ordinary phone company girl. No more and no less. That's the way it was.

I took the Sock Man's sock from my shoulder and looked it over for clues. It was an ordinary sock. It told me nothing. It wasn't new, but it was freshly laundered. What to do with this sock? I blushed to think of where it might have been. Then I rolled it up like a cinnamon bun and put it away in my purse.

By this time I'd officially stayed for the "second round," or maybe the "third round." I told myself that it was already so late that it didn't matter. Drew had no doubt already reached peak annoyance with me. Whether I rushed away now or stayed here with my friends a while longer would make no difference because when it came to Drew my goose was already cooked.

And so, I lingered. Now and then I tried to ask Randall Smiley to explain to me how he'd escaped from his sticky pickle under Vivienne Bianco's big bed, or why he'd gotten the boot, but whenever I tried to lob a question in his direction he'd cup his hand behind his ear and shake his head to indicate he had not heard me. We were a jolly noisy crowd. It was hard for me to hear Helen and she was just inches away. I forgot to wonder which round it was. I stayed on, and stayed on, until Meena noticed me and shouted above the cacophonous hum in the bar: "Celia! What are you still doing here? I made you a promise! I was supposed to pack you home hours ago!" and everybody decided at once that it was time to leave. It took us a long time to figure out how to split the bill seventeen ways. The math worked out poorly for our waiter, I think. And then we were all outside in a jumble, standing on the sidewalk, where I was surprised to learn it was late at night.

"Shit, the Sock Man is standing right over there, watching us," Helen said.

Poor Sock Man. We might have become friends under different circumstances. I didn't need to feel sorry for him long, it turns out, because a few weeks into the future he would become instantaneously famous all over the world after he jumped off the Golden Gate Bridge, and survived. From the papers I'd learn the Sock Man's true name, which was Lester Krebs. Lester would parlay his nearly successful suicide attempt into a trendy career, first invented in those times, known as "motivational speaker." Lester was one of the best. His speeches always began and ended in a flurried repetition of this single, perfect word: "Love! Love! Love! Love! Love!" And he would cry this one word out with feverish intensity while sweating profusely under stage lights, in a state of profound agitation that added to his mystique, and tens of thousands of people would take up the cry with tears in their eyes—"Love! Love! Love!"—and every so often I thought about showing up at one of Lester's speeches, or one of his book signings, either to return his sock or to see if he remembered me, but I never did.

"Come on, Celia, I'll hail you a taxi!" Randall boomed.

As soon as Randall stuck an arm out, a taxi appeared. Randall stuffed me inside. He was that kind of man. A big, booming, normal sort of guy who expected the world to conform to his expectations and was hardly ever disappointed.

SEVEN

HELLO, WIFE

I told the taximan I was late for a funeral which was a silly thing to say given the time of night but I guess he must have felt the customer is always right because he drove like a maniac and got me there in a blink. A man hopped aboard the train seconds after the conductor said "All aboard!" and sat himself down in the seat across from me. We were both breathing hard and we were sweaty. Even in my possibly booze-addled condition I couldn't help but notice that his suit fit him perfectly. I was intimately familiar with meticulous tailoring on account of my mother's sewing talent. A suit jacket should fit closely but not tightly. Sleeves should allow for a half inch of shirt cuff to peek out. Shoulders should crisply define the manly silhouette. I forgot to worry about Drew. I forgot to worry about how late it was. I remembered how I'd been expecting my one night out with the second-floor girls to change my life in amazing ways and it hadn't happened yet. We started off with a mighty jerk and it made the man's knees bump into my knees suggestively. The frozen margaritas were circulating in me. The Sock Man's venomous touch was also circulating. I discovered all sorts of naked thoughts in my head. I thought back on the advice I'd been given by those second-floor girls, who at some point that evening had urged me, in spirited drunken shouts, to find my pleasures wherever I pleased. Those girls had reminded me many times that my husband was not the boss of me. The well-tailored man's gaze accidentally connected with my gaze.

His eyes were entirely unshuttered. I felt cold, then hot. I looked away. I looked back. That is when I sadly discovered I'd made up a whole story about this man's interest in me, because in the brief interval when I'd broken my gaze, only to glance back flirtatiously moments later, the man had opened a briefcase on his lap. He had begun to shuffle the papers inside. He had grown absorbed in his own importance. I'd disappeared from his reality. My thoughts turned directionless. The frozen margaritas kept flinging new doors open in my head and the world was a blur. I heard the Crab Queen scuttling and tapping and rushing back and forth along the roof of the train car, trying to find her way in. I heard dogs barking, maybe inside my own head. To prove to myself I was sober, I tried to touch my finger to my nose, but my nose was too numb to feel anything, and the test was inconclusive.

When we came to the Belmont station the train screeched and shuddered to a halt. The doors didn't open right away. First a scratchy mechanical voice announced that a suicide leaper had leapt onto the tracks in front of the train ahead of us. It happens sometimes. A student fails a test and thinks he might as well end it. A spurned lover decides to make a statement so large that her former boyfriend will never be able to forget her. It disrupts the train schedule and upends travel plans. The scratchy voice told us we all needed to get out at this station. All of us passengers were forced to get off whether Belmont was our stop or not. Together we shuffled onto the bleak concrete platform, where the lights turned our skin sallow. Strangers formed an instantaneous bond and began to complain back and forth about the inconvenience.

"The same thing happened to me seven years ago," I heard somebody say. "No use waiting for the next train, it will take at least three hours and I'm talking best-case scenario."

I walked through the station and out the other side, where a different voice was coming through a different electronic bullhorn. This voice was inviting passengers to wait at the station for the suicide state of affairs to be cleared up after which the next train south would take us to our destination. Most people weren't buying that story. They were lining up at the pay phones to call home and ask someone to come collect them. There were pay phones in those days.

I was trying not to think about the poor splattered dead person lying in pieces for a mile or two along the tracks to the south. I've been told the train can't stop in time. The engineer sees a person standing on the tracks, illumined by the harsh train headlights from miles away. I have heard how the men who drive the trains are forevermore traumatized by the memory of seeing a soon-to-be-dead person standing in harm's way. Forever they are haunted by the image, and the knowledge that they caused the death of another. The engineer can't change fate no matter how quickly he slams on the brakes. The train will hit that suicidal person without a doubt and then it will continue to drag the body, or pieces of it, along for quite some distance. Weeks or years later a child or a homeless person will find a class ring with a finger bone still wearing it, there, along the tracks, all the fleshy parts picked off by carrion birds.

I wondered what to do. I didn't want to call Drew to ask him to come get me because I was already going to be in hot water with him, even before asking him for a favor. Then I remembered

Drew's car had dissolved in the night, and my mother's Oldsmobile was in the Redwood City municipal parking lot where I'd parked it that morning, so unless Drew had bought himself a new car already, he had no way to collect me. Next I thought about walking to the Redwood City train station on my own, to where my mother's Oldsmobile was waiting. The stations along this stretch of track were close together and it was probably only about a five-mile walk, I guessed. I could do it.

Or I could catch a bus.

Or I could wait for the next train. Waiting for the next train would get me home so late that Drew would be asleep when I got there, for sure, and he wouldn't wake up until morning, and there I'd be, snuggled next to him in bed, so cozily spooning in his arms that he'd forget all about how late I'd come home the night before, maybe.

As I stood there trying to work out the best plan for myself, I grew aware of the warm-kneed man standing next to me, and then I grew aware of the man's voice, saying softly in my ear, with his face so close that I could feel his warm breath on me: "This is my stop. My car is parked right over there. Can I give you a lift?"

And I knew, or thought I knew, that this man wasn't asking me this simple question out of the goodness of his heart, but even with this knowledge in me I heard myself reply: "If you could give me a ride to the Redwood City train station, I'd be grateful."

"You got it," he said.

I followed him to his car. It was one of those little Porsches. Although I am not one to be impressed by automobiles, I knew enough to know I was meant to be impressed by this one. The man unlocked the passenger-side door and then like a gentleman he took my hand and helped me into the seat. He walked around to his own side and got in. His car was a stick-shift vehicle. Whenever he shifted gears, I felt a powerful push-and-tug.

Just as we drove out of the parking lot, he asked me an unexpected question.

"Would you like to meet my new puppy?" he said.

I heard myself say, "Sure."

Blame those frozen margaritas. Blame the pep talk those second-floor girls had given me at some point, probably between the third and fourth rounds, or the fourth and fifth rounds, when they'd convinced me that women in bloodless marriages deserved to find their frisky pleasures elsewhere. Blame the time I was living through, a time when wife-swapping and hot tubs were first invented. Blame the knife in my boot. Blame the skittery, jittery defiance that welled up in me whenever I thought about Drew ramming me into a tree. Blame the Sock Man. Blame his sock. Blame the Crab Queen. Blame fear. Even in my fuzzy-drunk condition I knew for a fact that Drew was probably planning a bleak and escalatory lesson for me once I got home. What this warm-kneed man had in store for me was still a blurry mystery. I didn't know a thing about him. Not even his name. Maybe he just wanted to show me his new puppy. The man drove less than a mile before he turned into a driveway lined with giant oleander bushes. At the end of the driveway stood a house grand enough to warrant Corinthian columns in front. The house was made of white stone. It glinted in the dark.

The man pulled his car up and cut the engine. He came over to my side and opened the door and helped me out. I took his hand when he gallantly offered it. His gallantry struck me as false gallantry, showy and solicitous. His movements were too elaborate, almost maudlin, as if he thought treating me like a lady was a clever joke and he was the only audience. He led me up the big stone steps, and unlocked the front door, and we went inside. Before he found the light switch I heard the clickety-swift sound of a dog running on a shiny slippery floor in our direction. Then the man snapped on the light, and a huge space revealed itself, and a dog was bounding toward us in a deliriously goofy-puppy way. It was a young dog, but big. Its ears were enormous. The dog jumped on the man and tried to lick his face. There was dog-doo all over the place. That dog had been busy expressing its exuberant bowels all day. In places the dog had stepped in its own mess and tracked it elsewhere. When the man pushed the dog off, there were brown streaks on his suit jacket.

"Shit, shit, shit," the man said. "The goddamn dog-walker left the doggone dog room door open again! I've told her a hundred times to latch it tight!"

The man acted out his fury at the dog-walker by grabbing his dog roughly by the collar. He began to drag that dog to parts unknown. The dog didn't want to go. It sat on its haunches and slid along the shiny floor. I followed behind but when we came to a big kitchen I stopped and let the man and his dog struggle on without me. Although I was curious to see the "dog room" for myself—I was fascinated by the idea of a house being so roomy and luxurious that it had a designated dog room—I was even more interested in what I could learn from the stack of mail on the kitchen counter. The man still hadn't told me his name. Most of the envelopes were addressed to "Mr. and Mrs. Blake Goodman." I guessed from the available evidence that the man's name was Blake Goodman and that he was married. At the bottom of the stack there was a garden supply catalogue addressed to "Lavinia Goodman." I deduced that Lavinia was Blake's wife and that she liked to garden. I wondered where she was. Not expected home any-time soon, probably. Far away, I supposed. Maybe at a tractor convention in Des Moines.

Blake Goodman came back from where he'd been, without the dog. He'd left his suit jacket somewhere else, too. His shirt cuffs were monogrammed. The kitchen smelled like a poorly run shelter for indigent dogs because there was dog-doo in here, too, scattered in discrete piles all over the kitchen floor. That dog was apparently a well-fed dog.

I stopped thinking about the dog because Blake had begun to fondle me elaborately. However elaborate Blake's fondles were, they were mostly ineffectual, and I lost respect for him. He hadn't bothered to pick up the messes before starting in with the fondling. If I was going to go ahead and do things Drew had always accused me of doing, then Blake wasn't the one to do them with. I'd been snookered by my lack of experience with adultery, and by Blake's meticulous tailoring, and by his easy availability, only to learn to my great regret that this man was nothing but a dog-neglecter with poor fondling skills. From one second to the next, I went from a state of mind in which I was seriously contemplating my first adulterous act, to a state of mind where a voice next to my ear was screaming: "What are you thinking, get yourself out of here!" I've since discovered that many a human being has experienced such a tipping point, often after the profligate ingestion of alcohol, when what feels like a rush of uncontrollable lust transforms itself in an instant into a sad gaseous expulsion of said lust, a metaphorical "belch" of disappointment, one that leaves the body tired and the mind muddled. I'd just experienced this "belch" I'm talking about. And yet, here was this man. I was in this man's kitchen. This man had his hands on me. I was far from home and in need of a shower and a good night's sleep.

"You don't even know my name," I said.

He licked my ear.

"What's your name?" he said hoarsely.

"Joan," I said. "You were going to show me your new puppy."

"I showed you my new puppy," he said.

"You barely showed me your new puppy," I said.

He must have thought it in his best interest to humor me because he left and seconds later he came back with the dog. I could tell that dog had a good heart, but it had been sadly neglected in the love department. It craved attention. It had no manners. It was a hyperactive dog. It gave me the impression that it would one day grow up to be a German shepherd, a breed I'd adored ever since watching *Rin Tin Tin* at school as a child. My second-grade teacher used to play that old movie for us at recess time on rainy days. My teacher would drag the projector out of the utility closet and then one of the boys would be awarded the honor of threading the film through the projector in the prescribed manner. I was always jealous of those boys and their secret projector knowledge, a knowledge now lost in time, the way film projectors are lost in time, and films that come in flat metal canisters are lost in time. I gave Blake's dog some hearty nostalgic rubs. The dog thanked me by lolling out its tongue. I still had no idea how to get myself out of this poopy kitchen but it wasn't the dog's fault.

"What's your name?" I said to the dog.

"It's Ace," Blake said.

It was a bland and pointless name for a dog.

I reflected briefly on the oddness of this man telling me his dog's name and not his own name, which I secretly knew anyway.

"What do you think of my dog, Joan?" Blake said.

"I can see for myself that this dog has been sadly neglected in the love department," I said.

Blake laughed a rueful laugh.

"I would never neglect that dog," he said. "You should see that dog's pedigree. That dog's lineage goes all the way back to Horand von Grafrath. That dog is destined to sire champions!"

I had no witty answer ready for such a takedown as this and in the moment of silence that followed Blake started in again with his elaborate fondles.

"I don't like that," I said.

Blake grabbed the back of my head and pulled me to his waiting mouth and kissed me. Holy moly. Another tongue thruster. I didn't like it at all. I tried to pull away. He pushed me to my knees, and guided my head elsewhere. "Stop," I said. "Make me," he said. "Wait," I said. "Wait, wait, wait." I didn't say "stop" this time. "Stop" had already backfired on me. "Wait" didn't provoke him. "Wait" sounded like "Let me get you in the mood." He let go just enough for me to unsheathe my black knife from where it waited. "Stabbing" seemed too much of a statement. Instead, I chose a swift backhanded "slicing" gesture with the knife. It did the trick. I felt like a natural. Blame Dirk, my progenitor. Blake took a big step back. He looked down at his midsection, where a scarlet line—a line the color of blood, you might say—was slowly beading up.

"You stabbed me," he said incredulously.

"I did not stab you," I said.

Blake took a step toward me. The dog chose the side of right and without the slightest growl of warning bit down on a meaty part of his master's leg. His master shrieked. The dog let go.

Now the dog stood at the ready, by my side, baring his teeth and snarling a little snarl.

"Good doggo," I said.

"You bit me," the man said to the dog.

"It's just a flesh wound," I said. "Keep moving through it."

"You're crazy," he said.

"I'm not," I said.

I thought it was probably true that I wasn't crazy. I didn't feel crazy. Maybe Blake was the crazy one, for the way he thought it was A-OK to lure me into his home on the pretense of puppy love. I felt sane. I felt enlightened. So it comes to pass, for the Daughters of Dirk and the Minions of the Crab Queen, that one day we rip off our human masks and embrace the chaos.

I could tell Blake was no longer in the mood to give me a ride to the Redwood City train station and so I let myself out. I hated to leave that good old doggo behind. I was worried about that friendless dog's welfare, especially since he'd just bit down with some degree of force on his master's leg, but what could I do? I was in no position to save that dog. I still had some saving to do of my own self.

On the upside I felt confident Blake wasn't going to call the police on me anytime soon. Too much dog poop in the house. The police officers who came to investigate would be distracted by the messes. They would suspect Blake Goodman of animal abuse. They would grow suspicious, as one does of anyone who is unkind to a dog, and they would say: "Mr. Goodman, would you mind explaining to us again, please, what this young woman was doing in your house, at this hour, before the altercation began?"

Confident that my risk assessment of any pending police action against me was correct, I skipped merrily down the road toward home. It wasn't hard to know which way to go. I only needed to walk toward the silent hills to the west until my path intersected with El Camino Real, the route Spanish missionaries had laid out for me ever so long ago. Then I'd walk south for as long as it took, straight back to my mother's Oldsmobile in the municipal parking lot in front of the Redwood City station. I wasn't afraid. I had my black knife. What monsters lurked in the shadowed corners could tell I meant business and they left me alone. I felt tranquil, almost peaceful as I walked along. The moon was gibbous. The sky was awash with stars. I couldn't find Cancer, that faintest of zodiac constellations, but Cygnus was flying above my head and kept me company. My long walk was made lovelier by the time of dark I traveled through. I felt dangerous and animalistic. The thought of Drew made me snarl.

But as I made my way toward the time of my homecoming, the sky veiled itself with dewy mist, and my feelings flattened into dull dread. The night had been so full of unexpected happenings that I'd forgotten to worry about what lesson my husband might have in store for me when I got home. I tried to tell myself, "Hey, Celia. Drew is not the boss of you," but every step was bringing me closer to a reckoning. I didn't know how Drew would react when I got there. I'd never tested my boundaries so strenuously as on this night. And I had to admit that my recent behavior was not beyond reproach. I'd behaved like one of those fabled sheep that once they lose their way invariably end up eaten by wolves or walking sheeplike over the edge of a precipitous cliff to their doom. Eventually I had walked so long and so far that I was too tired to worry about such things, and when I saw my mother's Oldsmobile in the municipal parking lot, that car looked like a loyal friend who had resolved to wait for me, no matter how long it took.

What time was it by then? I had no idea. The town, the world, the houses on my street were dark and silent. I'd outlasted them all. I'd defeated my Drew. All the lights were out in the house. Drew had gone to bed. By morning he'd be less upset with me. He'd accept my apology. Drew's old car was gone and there was a new Ford Pinto parked in its place. The look of that car made me smile. Wasn't it just like my Drew to take care of his daily life challenges so efficiently? He hadn't gone out and bought himself a flashy sports car that would land us in debt forever. He'd chosen a solid economy car. In a rush of shame and gratefulness I remembered all the things I loved about the guy. My husband bought sensible cars. He enjoyed mowing the lawn. He made me happier than Blake Goodman ever could. Gratefully I put my house key in the lock and turned. The key turned, all right, but the door didn't budge. Because there was a brand-new slide bolt on the other side. Hastily installed there by my husband, just that night. A little loose, maybe. But effective even so. It was keeping me out. I remember thinking, even then, that Drew and I were having what amounted to a "heated conversation" about our differences. No more than that. It wasn't an argument. It was a tiff, maybe. A tit for tat, you might have called it. We were expressing our preferences to each other, the way married couples do. I'd expressed my preference to stay out late, by staying out late. He'd expressed his preference for his wife to come home when he told her to, by locking me out. I made my slow way along the perimeter of our house, trying every door and window. About halfway around the house, I noticed a Drew-shaped shadow inside. Drew was following my progress. Having a laugh or two at my expense, probably.

"Touché," I thought. "Well-played, husband."

Now that I had come all the way back around to the front door, I could feel Drew on the other side, waiting for me to knock and ring, and then to plead and cry. I didn't want to do any of those things. I'd sleep in my mother's Oldsmobile before I'd plead and cry. Better yet, I'd find another way in. The delinquents who had broken into the car at the station the other day inspired me. I walked next door. I dug out one of the distressed bricks that lined my neighbor's geranium bed and carried it back to the house. I broke one of the square windowpanes in the kitchen door and reached through and let myself in.

I snapped on the light.

Drew was in the kitchen. He was pointing a gun at me.

"What the hell, Celia!" he said.

And then? The roar of a gun—

Before I go on, allow me to step back, to a time when the bullet still rests peacefully inside that gun, because I want to share how I felt just before my husband pulled the trigger. I was flabbergasted. I was indignant. I'd spent the last couple of days thinking that, in the unlikely event I'd ever find myself in a domestic conflict ending in death, then I'd be like Gene Bianco. I'd be the raging wronged spouse who had finally had enough. I never imagined myself on the "dead victim" side of the equation. I was so sure I'd be like Gene Bianco in a domestic situation ending in death that for days I'd been rehearsing the role. I'd been getting in touch with my hidden rages. I'd chosen my weapon. I'd had a practice skirmish that same night. Only to learn, here at this penultimate moment, that I was the soon-to-be-dead victim of domestic violence all along, and not the raging, wronged spouse.

As these bright revelations cascaded over me like a cold spring shower, I came to a precious moment in life that not all humans are privileged to reach. In that skinny interval between the time my husband said *What the hell, Celia!* and the time the gun roared, I came to understand that I was about to die. I, Celia, was about to become the next Vivienne Bianco, only without the smutty fun before the end. Does the woman in this scene have regrets? Oh yes, my dears. So many regrets. So many lousy choices. This night was supposed to have been her one wild exploratory break from all the weighted expectations Drew had layered atop of her like so many layers of troweled concrete. She'd bungled it badly. She would have been better off going home with the Sock Man. She would have been better off submitting to Blake Goodman's goonish pawing. She would have been better off committing all the ripe promiscuous acts her husband has accused her of every day of their married lives. She would have been better off if she had driven out of that parking lot three days ago and followed the open road.

But of course I wasn't thinking of any of these things before my husband pulled the trigger. I'm embellishing. I'm adding this-and-that, after the fact, to prolong the moment, and to make it more dramatic. It would be more accurate to tell you that my brain was flushed clean, and my body was filled with cold sludge, and I might as well have already been a dead cold slab of meat empty of all thought and intention since there was so little going on in my head. Except for the fear. The fear was all-consuming.

But also of course these further remarks I've recorded about the state of my brain and body, and about the fear I must have surely felt, as my husband pointed a gun at me and squeezed, are as inaccurate as my former claims that I was standing there, frozen in the moment, thinking long thoughts about how I would have been better off going home with the Sock Man, or submitting to Blake Goodman's needy fondles, or following the open road—all of these studied observations about my regrets being intentionally fashioned long after the night when my husband fired that gun, as I try to recall, and to put into words, what it's like to reach a tipping point between love and death, just before a bullet is about to rip through your innards, after which you will be utterly and irrevocably dead, hideously transformed into a tragic statistic, to be talked about, at best, for a few short days, in a handful of earnest discussions around a sticky square table in the designated break room for smokers at your former workplace, or in a few gossipy conversations between neighbors on your street, who when you were alive did no more than wave at you blandly as they were backing their cars out of their driveways, but now that you have met your grisly end, these formerly aloof neighbors will be energized by your smarmy death, and will be talking over fences about it, and be on the telephone with distant friends even before the detectives have left the scene, and will say to these friends, in hushed excited whispers: *Shot to death! Right across the street! Such a sweet young girl! You can never know what's happening behind closed doors—*

"What the hell, Celia!" Drew said.

And then? The roar of the gun—

Only guns don't really "roar," do they? I know that now. Contrary to the story Randall Smiley regaled us with in the designated break room for smokers, a gun doesn't "roar." A gun makes no sound at all. Or at least it makes "no sound at all" when you're about to catch a bullet in your gut. I didn't hear a peep. Not until long after the bullet had met its target, and by then the sound the gun made was a dim memory, if that.

And what is even more remarkable is the way that gunshot made no sound at all in the opinion of my neighbors. Not one of those neighbors did more than wake up just enough to ask themselves: "Was that a gunshot?" before they turned themselves over in bed like plump sausages on a griddle and went back to sleep. That's how it is.

"Hello, wife," Drew said. "I almost shot you. I could have shot you. I thought you were a housebreaker."

My husband seemed calm to me, given the circumstances. The bullet had missed me, sure, but not by enough to explain my husband's eerie equanimity. I couldn't understand his easy calm. I couldn't understand how he'd missed me, either. Drew was a crack shot and he'd missed me by a good six inches. A new hole in the wall behind me had begun to send out spidery cracks in the plaster.

"I really could have shot you," Drew said. "Legally, I mean."

"Oh," I might have said.

"I could have shot you dead. I wake up in the middle of the night and somebody is at the window, trying to break in. I grab my weapon. It's one in the morning. My home is under attack. I hear the sound of glass breaking in the kitchen. Somebody has broken into my house! Maybe they're here to kill me! I shoot first. Before the guy shoots me. That is my right. I have the legal right to defend my home. A man's home is his castle, and my castle has been breached!"

"Drew," I said.

He waved the gun in his hand around lackadaisically.

"I'm talking, Celia," he said. "What a tragic mistake! It's not a bad man lying dead on the kitchen floor! It's my slutty wife, breaking into her own house at one in the morning! Poor wife! Lying here dead on the floor! Here she is! Dead!"

About then it dawned on me that Drew was way ahead of me. Imagine a man disgruntled about his wife's tardiness. She has stayed out past her appointed hour. She is so late that he has decided to craftily install a slide bolt on the front door. Not because he wants his wife to plead and cry to be let in. Not because he expects his wife to sleep in her car, like a defeated loser. He knows his wife. She is the kind of wife who will grab a distressed brick from next door, and will smash a window-pane, and will break into her own house rather than let her husband win—and there he will be, eager to give his slutty wife the scare of a lifetime and to teach her a lesson she will never forget, by shooting the wall behind her ear. After this night, his wife will never be confused about who is boss in this house. She will never again come home a single slim minute past the expected minute.

“I’m sorry,” I said.

“Oh no!” Drew said. “That’s not some sleazy burglar lying dead on the kitchen floor! It’s just my slutty wife!”

“The train hit somebody,” I said. “Somebody was standing on the tracks. It fouled up the schedule. It took hours to clean up. It was an awful situation—”

Drew wasn’t listening. He was busy taking in the state of my clothes. I’d just noticed, myself, that my clothes were in an incriminating state of disarray. If you were to say that I looked like I’d been fondled a time or two that night then you would not be wrong. And I felt shame. I felt such terrible shame. I had wronged my Drew. He had put down the gun by then. Now the gun was resting on the kitchen counter. It was my own little .38 Special. Drew was spinning that gun around on the counter in a reckless way that probably wasn’t part of the safety protocols his father had taught him. Then he looked at me wistfully. His wistful look gave me hope that he’d decided to forgive me.

“Let me show you something, wife,” he said.

He held his hand out. I took it. He led me by the hand to the door of the pantry, where I kept my Barbie doll collection, and opened it. He snapped on the light. Oh. Every box, torn open. Dolls in a heap on the floor. Their clothes, like mine, in disarray. Or altogether missing. Dismembered dolls. Heads. Legs. Naked torsos. Dolls posed obscenely. Sucking one another’s plastic breasts. Scissors-fucking. Ass-fucking.

“Someone must be really upset with you,” Drew said.

“Drew—”

“What? Are you going to tell me you’re sorry?”

“No,” I said.

"Are you going to cry?"

I felt so tired.

"I'm going to bed," I said.

"Is that right?" Drew said. "Are you going to bed, Celia? Is that what you're going to do? Are you going to bed?"

Drew began to strong-arm me in his own special way, straight to the chest with the heel of his hand. Not hard. Almost gently. Again. Again. He wouldn't let me get by. Eons have passed beyond memory since that day. Dynasties have fallen to dust. And still my nineteen-year-old self can't answer my simplest questions. I want to reach right through the years and shake that girl by the shoulders and say, *You stupid ninny! Why didn't you tell someone? Why didn't you ask for help?* Or better yet: *Why didn't you defend yourself, when your black knife had proven itself that same night!*—but that girl is having none of my pious lectures. Indignantly, she reaches back out to me across the years and gives her old wizened self a few clarifying slaps. Then she says to me: You're *the stupid one, you infirm old hag. Now listen to me! This man was our husband. We were his wife. We'd made a promise. And those three words acted like a binding spell on us, as well you remember.* Husband. Wife. Promise. *We are the same person, you and I!*

And it's true. She was me, and I am she, and together we have come to a moment that never ends for either of us, and is never in the past, and our husband has just shot the wall next to our ear, and now our husband is pushing us in the chest, again, again—and we forget to have an opinion about it. Our mind goes blank. Oh yes, my dears. I feel it still. The hollow thump to my chest. The emptiness inside. The certainty that I deserve it.

But then something new happens between this husband, this wife. A small thing. Barely worth mentioning. What happens is this: The wife shoves back. Wait a minute. *Shove* is a gross exaggeration of the facts. It's a stupid small gesture. More "slap" than "shove." More "gentle touch" than "slap." In another context the same gesture would be a sign of affection. Whatever it is, the gesture surprises the husband, and he, in turn, makes a nearly imperceptible change in the pressure of his own hand, right there, right in the middle of his wife's chest, and the change is just enough for his wife to lose her balance—and even this loss of balance is probably not the man's fault—it could be her own fault, because she is tipsy, and because she is tired—and she slips and sits down hard on the pantry floor.

The door slams shut.

She hears him turn the key.

"Drew," she says. "Come on."

The light goes out.

Here she sits, in the dark, surrounded by dead Barbie dolls.

She hears her husband's voice, rasping, from the other side of the locked pantry door.

"Now you're in for it, Celia," the voice says.

EIGHT

SMALL PLASTIC LIVES

So I fluffed up all the Barbie doll clothes I could find in the dark and put my purse on top of the pile, to make myself a little pillow, where I laid down my head and went to sleep.

Okay, maybe it was not exactly "sleep" I went to. Maybe it was more like I experienced a catatonic reaction to getting shot at, then locked inside a narrow pink pantry with fifty-seven desecrated Barbie dolls. It was maybe more like that. And maybe I didn't fall into that catatonic sleep right away. There were moments of panic and rage and still more panic to live through before I fell into that catatonic stupor I'm talking about. I tried to gauge how long I could last in the pantry before I expired. My first instinct was to think Drew wasn't going to unlock that door anytime soon. He'd probably leave me in here at least until I peed or soiled myself, to teach me a lesson. What Drew didn't know is that I couldn't be shamed that way. Not any longer. I'd learned from Doggo's example. I would never again let myself be shamed by my body, or its functions, or its urges.

I kicked at the pantry door a few times, experimentally. The door was solid wood. I soon gave up on the idea of kicking it down. Could I pick the lock? I had no idea how to pick a lock. I considered the door hinges. As soon as the words *door hinges* came into my head, the fifty-seven desecrated Barbie dolls at my feet all perked up, and urged me on—*Yes! Consider the door hinges!*—and although it would have been much more satisfying to me, personally, to kick the door down with my own two boots than to figure out a clever way to remove the door from its hinges, I thought the Barbie doll heads were probably right.

Then I realized, through touch alone, because it was dark in there, that the door opened the other way, out into the kitchen, and naturally the hinges were on the other side of that door, and unavailable to me, and so the door-hinges idea was also a bust, and I was out of ideas, and so I fluffed up all the Barbie doll clothes I could find in the dark and put my purse on top of the pile to make myself a little pillow, where I laid down my head and went to sleep.

I didn't think another thought until the next morning, when I woke up with the stark conviction in my head that I was a hermit crab and I'd just outgrown my old shell with a vengeance. I also woke up with a crick in my neck, and to an open pantry door. The pantry door wasn't just unlocked. It was swung wide open. It enraged me to think of Drew skulking back at some point, opening that door, and gazing down on me, sprawled there, catatonically asleep and helpless.

It crossed my mind about then that I hated my husband. I walked through the house like a snarling beast, looking for Drew, and didn't find him. He wasn't anywhere. His gun safe was open. My little .38 Special was missing, and some of the long guns. That is when I unexpectedly thought back on my mother's sewing lessons. I'd never been much of a seamstress because I found the work tedious. But an idea had just come to me for a new sewing project, and so I pulled my mother's dusty sewing machine out from a closet and threaded it. My idea was to fashion a sturdy leather sheath for my dirk. I borrowed the material I needed from Drew's beloved leather jacket. For once I didn't mind the tedium of the task. I loved the way the needle looked as it made hundreds of small punctures in the rich leather of my husband's former jacket. When I was done I girded my loins with my dirk. My black knife still rested in my boot. I felt powerful and courageous and ready for the good fight until I glanced at myself in the bathroom mirror. What I saw did not bring me confidence. I looked ridiculous. Who was I fooling? What was the point in fighting back, anyway? Just look what had happened to Gene Bianco. He had fought back and now he was a sad broken incarcerated sack of a man who would spend his life in jail for murder. That would be his best option. Probably he'd be sent to the gas chamber.

As for me, I was no killer. I was barely angry at Drew by then. I'd used up all my fury while I was cutting his leather jacket up into pieces to make a sheath for my dirk. What could my little hands do to save me? Nothing. "Calm yourself, Celia," I said to myself. "Be sensible. You have got to get out of this mood of yours, and curb your killer instincts, before somebody dies."

And so I put those knives away, both of them, in my secret place.

I put my glory-dreams of fighting my way out of my troubles away, too.

Then I called in to the floor supervisor's line at work.

The floor supervisor on duty that day was Herbie LaDue, and he was one of the good ones. I told him I'd been in a serious car accident. It was accurate, though belated, information.

"Oh, honey, take the whole day off," he said.

I said: "Oh no, Mr. LaDue, it isn't necessary for me to take the whole day off. I'll be in as soon as I can get there this morning."

"Well, honey, if that's really what you want to do, then I have to say we could use the help," he said.

It *was* what I wanted to do. Out here in the world I was at the mercy of my most dangerous instincts. What I needed was routine. I yearned for the steady flow of other people's voices and other people's problems in my ear. Just before I left for the train station I decided to call Augusta. Even though Augusta was not my favorite person, we had something in common, which was that we both loved her son. I wanted to see if she had any intelligence to share about Drew's whereabouts and well-being.

"You have some nerve calling here," Augusta said.

"I was wondering if you'd heard from Drew lately," I said.

"My son came back home this morning," she said. "He's sleeping. He told me everything, Celia."

What did Augusta mean by "everything"? Did it include the news that her son had shot a gun at me the night before, and had desecrated my fifty-seven Barbie dolls, and had locked me in a pink pantry overnight? I wondered about it. Fortunately, Augusta was in the mood to explain what "everything" meant, from her perspective.

"He's finally come clean about you, Celia," Augusta said. "The way you come home drunk in the morning. The way you sleep around with God knows who. You demean him. You take away his manhood. It's sick. You're sick. You marry the best guy in the world and you treat him like dirt."

"Okay, okay, okay," I said.

"It's a blow to a mother's gut to see her son treated like dirt," she said. "Believe me, it's a blow."

"I wouldn't say he's perfect," I said.

"How crazy can you be?" Augusta said. "Accusing your own husband of breaking into your car. Accusing your own husband of calling you and harassing you at work. Do you believe these things? Or do you like to torture your husband with made-up accusations? He's driving up to Chico today. He's going to stay with Rick until he sorts things out for himself. I keep telling him to cut you loose, but will he listen? I doubt it. After all the ways you abuse him, he says he loves you. My son is too good to see the bad in you."

Rick was Drew's friend from high school. He'd been Drew's best man. They'd been on the track team together. Back in the day, Rick had thrown the javelin. He went hunting with Drew sometimes. At our wedding he'd leaned in as if to give me a kiss and had stuck his tongue in my ear instead and ever since I'd been wary around him. What was it about men and their tongues? Anyway, Drew was going to Chico. Chico was a four-hour drive at least. Drew would drive away in his new Ford Pinto, and when he came home, he'd be less unhappy with me. I felt myself let go of a big feeling. All my bones and stress went away. I opened my mouth. Maybe to say something in my defense. Maybe to apologize for treating Drew like dirt. Before I could decide, the chance was over.

"My son isn't dirt," Augusta said. "*You* are the dirt, Celia. That's exactly what you are. Dirt! Dirt! Dirt! Dirt! Don't call here again."

Augusta hung up.

The phone rang.

I answered it.

"Drew?" I said.

"Celia," Drew said. "What was I thinking? I can't think at all when you're around. I love you so much—"

I heard tragic, contritional sobs.

"I love you. I love you," Drew said. "I'm sorry. Oh, honey, I'm so sorry."

Drew was apologizing. That was new. That had honestly never happened, not in my life. My instincts began to fly in a whole new direction, away from my former chaotic indignation at the way he had shot a bullet at me and toward the idea of reconciliation and forgiveness. I, Celia, had the power to make things right. My husband had given me that power. He had asked for my forgiveness. I remembered why I loved him. I felt myself fill up with warmhearted thoughts about the guy. Then my eyes happened to glance up at the bullet hole in the kitchen wall. The cracks in the plaster had pulled apart in the night, and there was crumbly stuff collecting on the floor over there. Maybe at this very second I was being contaminated by asbestos. Lately the papers had been peppered with stories of former asbestos workers developing hideous tumors on their lungs.

"Celia?" Drew said.

"Look, sweetheart," I said. "You shot a bullet at me. You locked me in the pantry."

"You know I missed on purpose!" he said.

"Be that as it may," I said. "I need some space and time. Away from you. I need to think. I think it's a good idea you go see Rick. Stay in Chico with Rick. I'll call you tonight. Say hi to Rick for me. We'll talk tonight."

"Why are you being this way?" Drew said. "You know I missed on purpose!"

"Get off that phone, honey! Why are you speaking with that strumpet!" I heard Augusta say.

"I love you," Drew said.

"Don't worry," I said. "I know you missed on purpose."

As we said good-bye we made small kissing noises into the phone. I loved him. I loved him, sometimes. I loved the idea of him being far away in Chico. I couldn't decide how I felt about him. I loved him, probably. I loved the way I'd have the house to myself tonight, because I, Celia Dent, had told Drew what to do, and he had listened.

Before I left the house for work, I walked all around and into every room, touching things. My mother's dear presence was all over this house. I had never mourned her properly, it seemed to me. I'd let myself get swept up in whatever drama of the day came along between Drew and me. It occurred to me I was in the wrong job. My job was always stirring up my most chaotic instincts. I decided that after Drew and I made up, and after he found a job as a scrub tech at a place that hadn't fired him for insubordination yet, I'd talk to him about whether I could quit the phone company for good. Maybe I'd work in a notions store instead. A notions store would be a much better place for an excitable girl like me. Instead of listening to angry voices pouring into my ear I'd spend my days helping women pick out buttons and ribbons and zippers for their latest sewing projects. In a year, or maybe two, Drew and I would add a baby to the mix. I would be a good wife. I would be a good mother. In the meantime I wanted my days to be as uneventful as days could ever be. I craved routine. I wanted to be bored.

As soon as I got to work Herbie LaDue strode over to my workstation from his dais to shake my hand and to thank me for coming in. He told me I was brave to come to work in spite of having suffered from a serious car accident and that it showed I had gumption. I said thanks. I felt like a fraud, though, because I'd kept moving through the pain and my ribs were barely tingling by then. As I began to answer calls I noticed a new person sitting in Randall Smiley's old spot. She had her headset on. She was smiling and looking as if she was listening intently. She looked ready to solve her customers' problems because it was her job to be a problem-solver. I thought back on my first days as a billing operator. In the beginning, I'd foolishly imagined I could reach through the telephone wires and help my customers resolve their complicated financial situations. I'd felt like the Florence Nightingale of the Resident Billing Office. I believed those customers. I believed their sorry tales. All too soon the scales fall from our eyes. We discover how easily people prey on our sympathetic instincts. They lie to us. We become embittered, petty people ready to rip lips left and right. We end up being skeptics about the human condition and we harden our hearts against those who deserve our forbearance and pity. And I did not like the bitter person I had become, either at home or at work. I resolved to do better than bitter, and to treat each call as an opportunity to spread hope and humanity. It was one of those mornings when I agreed willy-nilly to whatever zany extensions on their billing dates my customers asked for. On this day, the customer was king.

When my lunch break came along, I wanted to avoid running into any of those second-floor girls because I felt ashamed of the way I'd conducted myself the night before at the St. Francis Hotel. Not to mention all the mischief I'd caused later in the night. No luck. The elevator stopped on the second floor and Helen stepped in. About then it occurred to me, though, that Helen was someone I didn't mind running into.

"Celia," she said. "How about that Sock Man."

"How about that Sock Man," I said.

"You want to go out for a bite with me somewhere?" she said.

"All right," I said.

We ended up going to the dim sum place around the corner. Dim sum is a good bet when you're with somebody. It's not such a good bet when you're alone. You end up needing to eat three or six of something, instead of one or three of something. The whole concept of having many different sorts of tasty snacks for lunch is defeated by the need to eat so many of the same kind. They never let you order just one of a thing. You need to order three, or six. You fill yourself up with sameness long before it's time for sweet sesame balls.

Helen poured me some tea.

"I'm thinking maybe I want to kill my husband," I said.

Helen looked thoughtful.

"I'm not sure that's such a good idea," she said. "You might get away with it, but probably you won't, and you'll end up going into one of those maximum-security places, and if they put you in one of those maximum-security places, how would I ever get to know you? How would we ever have another dim sum lunch? How would we ever stay friends if you made me drive to one of those maximum-security places to see you? The guards would pat me down each time. I like you, Celia, but I don't know if I could go through those pat-downs on a weekly or even a yearly basis."

"Okay, yeah, I can see your point of view," I said. "Anyway, it was just a thought."

"No, I get it. I totally get it," Helen said.

We went on eating dim sum as if no conversation about my possible plan to kill my husband had ever been discussed by us, not even in the most lighthearted of ways. Helen and I were the best possible dim sum partners because we liked the same things. Helen ate wolfishly. She scraped the last kernel of sticky rice out from its leaf-wrapper and snapped it up with wolfish attention. I liked her manner of degustation. Her approach to food and maybe life itself was wild and lustful. We kept ordering those precious little dim sum dishes until we'd stuffed ourselves silly and the stack of plates on our table was so high it was teetering and about to topple over.

Helen and I fought over the third sesame ball until the server came over and neatly cut it in half for us, with her special sesame-ball-cutting scissors.

When the bill came, Helen grabbed it.

"I'm paying," she said. "That way, you'll need to ask me out again one day to return the favor."

"Thank you," I said.

We were so full of good flavors that it felt wrong to us both to trudge straight back to work, but I would have done just that if Helen hadn't blurted out another idea.

"We should call in sick," she said.

"Okay," I said.

There was a pay phone on the corner. Helen called in first, to the supervisor's line on the second floor. She told her supervisor a colorful story about a nasty intestinal bug that had just sprung up in her body. She added a convincing sound effect or two. My call in to the third-floor supervisor's line was easy. I already had a sympathetic listener in Herbie LaDue. He said, "Sure, oh, sure, Celia, I told you not to push it, a car accident is a serious thing, take tomorrow off, too, if you need it," and that was that.

"What do we do now?" I said.

"I know exactly what we're going to do," Helen said.

"What's that?" I said.

Helen said she didn't want to tell me yet. She said I should just trust her, and follow her. I said I would. I followed her for eight or ten twisty, rambling blocks, until the shops disappeared and all that was left lining the streets were former factories and warehouses with graffiti splayed across their sides. Decades into the future those buildings would be converted into executive apartments. Young tech entrepreneurs would move in. They would keep all the pipes exposed, and the industrial light fixtures intact, for authenticity, and their furniture would be made out of black leather and chrome. Oh yes, my dears, those days to come would be giddy days, but here in 1974, where I currently found myself scurrying after Helen—who was small and quick, and hard to keep up with—most of those buildings were still eyesores.

We came to a place with recently cleaned windows in front and a hand-painted sign above the double-doors, and the sign said: TRAMPOLINE SCENE.

"I come here sometimes after work," Helen said, and opened the door.

A shapely man sat behind a desk. Helen handed him a card and he punched it.

"And this here is my guest," she said.

"Okay, Helen," the shapely man said, and punched the card another time.

We walked through a pair of wooden swinging doors, into a room of men working on their muscles and where the air was ringing with the clang of weights. Helen didn't stop there. We walked straight through another pair of doors. Here we were in a room full of trampolines. No one was in there but us.

"Come on," Helen said.

She took her shoes off and climbed up and began to jump. I did the same. Something was springing inside of me—spring flowers, the sound of rain, a friend who made me smile. My body, moving through space. An unraveling of every clenched muscle and from all the years I'd spent tensing myself into shapes that kept me safe. Here was Helen, undoing me, like a shot of whiskey. Like a bolt of lightning. Like fiery confetti. For the longest time we were the only ones in there, in a space with sixteen trampolines and thick mats on the floor. The walls were brick and soaringly high on every side. We kept flying toward the high ceiling until we were flying for real. As I jumped, I was transfixed by the little gestures Helen made with her fingers, on the way up and on the way down. We jumped for a long time. Me, she, me, she. At first our hair was flying up loose above our heads but after a while our hair looked like seaweed-tendrils sticking to our sweaty foreheads. I was feeling a strong feeling. I wasn't ready to define it. Wild, maybe. Uninhibited, maybe. Then two men came into the room and I felt shy again. Those men began to jump together, while holding hands, and a new thought came into my head: Was I falling in love with Helen? Absolutely not. I rejected the idea. For one thing, I was married. But: Here was Helen. Her smile made me feel as if I were part of nature, not a flawed human being. No one thinks a tree isn't beautiful. No one thinks a craggy hill is ugly just because it's craggy, either. That's the way Helen made me feel. Like a tree on a craggy hill. I stopped fretting for maybe a second or two. Something flew off of me. An old feeling. An old skin. That's when I noticed every crick and creak and pang of pain in my body was gone and I felt like a fluttery flag. I'd moved through it completely, thanks to Helen.

We stopped jumping, both at once.

We climbed off the trampoline and lay down on our backs on the padded floor.

Panting. A little dizzy.

We looked up at the ancient high ceiling with its warehouse-bright light fixtures.

"That's what I'm talking about," Helen said.

I looked at my watch.

"Helen," I said. "I need to be on the next train or I'm toast."

Helen didn't argue. She didn't try to talk me out of it.

"Come on, I'll come with you to the station," she said. "Let's run."

Even if Drew was in Chico, four hours away, I was worried he'd be calling me every six minutes to check on whether I was home from work on time. Helen and I ran all the way to the station and somehow got there just as the conductor was stepping on board and waving to the engineer, far ahead, to get on with it. It happened a long time ago. I like to imagine Helen gave me a kiss before I jumped on that train. It's highly unlikely that she did, because she was busy asking herself the same, entirely unexpected question I had asked myself recently—was she falling in love with me?—and it would take us both a good half dozen years to answer that question for ourselves in the affirmative. That's the way it is sometimes. We can take forever to arrive at the most obvious truths about ourselves, because the will to conform is mighty in us, and the fear of somebody finding out we're not normal is a mighty fear.

But even if Helen probably didn't kiss me that afternoon, I'm still certain there was something else, something lovely about the way she said good-bye to me—if not a kiss, then a fragile open look, or a silent promise, and maybe—yes, here is the way I want to remember it, and since it happened long ago, and since there is no longer anyone left alive who can contradict me, I will tell it *this* way: After Helen said good-bye to me she stood on the platform as I took my seat in the train car, and until the train began to move we waved back and forth crazily, both of us with chests heaving from our run, both of us gathering gulpfuls of air into our lungs, and as the train pulled away, Helen followed, waving, walking swiftly along, and then she broke into a run to keep up, all the while waving like a young bride seeing her fellow off to war, which was the sort of movie I was particularly fond of in those days—but eventually the train pulled away and left Helen behind and I was alone. Except I wasn't alone. Because everyone in the car was looking at me, and they were smiling, and they were asking themselves: "Who *is* this girl with the rosy cheeks, and why is she glowing, and where can I get me some of that feeling?" This is true. I had made a train full of people all smile back at me, and I felt as if I had just discovered in myself a new and precious power.

When I got home I was shocked to discover that the phone wasn't ringing with Drew on the other end demanding to know where I'd been.

I dialed Rick's number in Chico.

"Hello?"

"Drew!" I said.

"This is Rick," Rick said. "Good God, Celia. You've broken his balls. You're a ball-breaker. What is it with you?"

"I'm sorry," I said.

"He doesn't want to talk," Rick said.

"Let me speak to my husband," I said.

"Give it," I heard Drew say.

"Drew?"

"It's Drew," Drew said. "I've been calling all evening. Where have you been?"

There was a catch in his throat that endeared him to me.

"Shit, Drew, it's six-thirty, that's the time I always get home," I said.

It startled me mightily to hear how much I didn't sound like myself. For one thing, I'd never said the words *shit* and *Drew* in the same sentence before. Helen swore like a stevedore and her vernacularisms had worn off on me. For another thing, my voice was full of unaccustomed joy, on account of the afternoon I'd spent with a new friend.

"You sound different," Drew said. "Is somebody there with you?"

"Nobody," I said.

Which was true, but it sounded like a sneaky lie even to me.

"When are you coming home?" I said in my defense. "I miss you."

I missed him. All that tramping with Helen had put me in a forgiving mood.

"Do you really miss me?" Drew said. "Do you really? I don't know. You were the one who sent me away. And now you've changed your mind. Well, isn't that just great. I think you should miss me longer. I think you should have a good long time to miss me. You can use the time to think about what a miserable life you'd be living, Celia, without me in the picture."

"I love you," I said.

"Do you?" Drew said. "I wonder."

"Gimme that phone, brother," I heard Rick say.

"Celia," Rick said into my ear. "Just leave the man alone. He's not coming back. He's never going to speak to you again."

Then dial tone.

After Rick hung up, I went into the kitchen and made myself some mac and cheese. When I was done eating, I cleaned up. Eating and cleaning are two things that have a way of absorbing all thoughts beyond the simple task at hand. The chewing. The swallowing. The making of warm sudsy water in the sink. The slow round washing of the dinner plate, with the sponge, to be followed by the drying. One side effect of industrialization is an explosion of despair. Back in the day, when all labor was menial labor, we humans never had time to fret over our own despair. Now we have plenty of free time and we use our time to ponder the pain and meaninglessness of our fragile existences, but none of those dark thoughts could touch me that night because I occupied myself with the eating, and the dish-cleaning, the dish-drying, and when I was done with those pleasant menial tasks, I decided it was time to clean up the broken sad pile of desecrated Barbie dolls in the pantry.

I opened the pantry door.

There they were, those sad ruined Barbies, sucking on each other's hairless hard naked crotches.

I said to them: "Poor Barbies, poor things!—your best days are over."

But the dolls vociferously disagreed. They shook their rubbery heads and declared, *Oh no, Celia, you've got it all wrong! Don't pity us. Not ever! We have been liberated from our boxes! We have come to know passion! Oh yes, my dear—see how our small plastic lives have burned so very brightly!*—and I saw that it was true. Here before my eyes was a tale of love and death all over again, but in miniature. Now their stories had come to an end. Since the next day was trash day, I gathered them up lovingly into a brown grocery bag. When I was through scooping them into the bag, I stuffed their broken bodies into the trash can and I carried the can to the curb. Rest in peace, my small plastic friends.

I went back inside, back into my warm, bright kitchen, where I put one finger in the bullet hole in the wall. As hard as I tried, I couldn't feel the bullet. My finger wasn't long enough or skinny enough to reach it. Since I couldn't touch it for myself, it didn't feel real to me. This bullet in the wall felt more like a movie prop. The movie I found myself in felt like a rollicking comedy of manners, the kind of movie where a couple of crazy kids keep fighting about things that don't really matter until they learn a valuable lesson and fall in love all over again in the end.

As for me, I'd just told my husband that I loved him. *That* felt real. Not this bullet in the wall. Maybe you know what I'm talking about. Maybe you've also known the thrill of loving somebody the way I loved my Drew. This person you love is fragile and incomplete. All the time, he's thinking he is the strong one, but you know better. The truth is, he's scared, and scarred, and he can't live without you. So you swoop in. You build him up. By making him feel strong, you prove to yourself that you are the strong one. You feel so good about your selflessness. The feeling carries you through the bad patches. Only you can see the truth about this man of yours—that he's helpless without you. You respond to him the way you'd respond to your own child. And you call this feeling "love." It's a powerful feeling. It makes you stay. Don't you feel the truth of it? Don't you see? I wasn't the victim. I was the rock. Whenever I was on the brink of understanding my life any differently from this, my Drew would say something beautiful to me. His words would persuade me. He would say: *I need you. Without you, I'm nothing.* Here was a man who had shot a bullet at me. Who had rammed me into a tree. Who had called me disgusting, many times. Who had strong-armed me casually whenever he thought I needed to be taught a lesson.

Who had locked me in a pink pantry overnight, and who had raped me a time or two—my mind, unconvinced, interrupts me here to say, "Oh, Celia, don't catastrophize; rape is such a judgmental word, when you know he never left bruises"—and all the worries I'd ever felt about the man would suddenly feel exaggerated and overblown in my head, and any complaints I might have felt about him seemed trivial and insignificant, because he needed me, and because I loved him—and that is why I knew that, in a day or maybe two, Drew would ask me once more to forgive him—and when he did, I would say: "Oh no, Drew, you got it all wrong, I'm the one who needs to be forgiven," and I would tell him how sorry I was, and I'd promise to love him better next time.

NINE

LOVE AND DEATH

Days and days and days went by without me hearing a peep from my Drew, until our argument seemed foolish and remote. My memory of the way Drew had looked at me, just before he'd shot a bullet into the wall, had by then dissolved into a nearly-forgotten dream. I dialed Rick's number every night. No answer. I began to think Drew had been convinced to leave me by his good pal Rick, with the help of Augusta, who had always thought of me as an opportunistic skank. Other times I told myself that Drew and Rick had probably gone hunting. Drew was probably out there in the manly wilderness, letting off steam, shooting his guns at things he didn't need to miss on purpose. When he felt better, he would come home to me. I longed to smell him, all pine soap and antiperspirant. He'd bring me flowers when he came home. Or venison steaks. Sometimes when Drew was upset with me, he'd disappear like that, right off the map, and come home with a wild pig or a stag or some other dead thing tied to the roof of his car. I kept telling myself it was one of those times.

One morning at work I found myself stepping into the same elevator as Helen. We hadn't spoken since the afternoon of dim sum and trampolines. The elevator was crowded and there were people standing between us but Helen caught my eye. "Are you all right?" she said. I didn't know what to answer. Maybe it was just a throwaway comment on her part. In that case I could shrug and smile and that would be that. But maybe Helen really wanted to know if I was all right. In that case I could have told her I was still troubled by the way I'd been fondled by a well-tailored man, after which I'd sliced him neatly open with an illegally concealed "black knife." Or I could have shared with her how unsettled I still felt whenever I thought about the way my husband had shot a bullet at me not so long ago. Or I could have kept it lighter, but still friendly, by telling Helen that my husband was away and I missed him, or that I'd recently given up on my hobby of collecting Barbie dolls, or that I hadn't taken a shower in quite some days. These would have all been fine, true things to say to Helen in an elevator but I couldn't decide what level of sharing was best. Under the circumstances, "Are you all right?" sounded like a trick question. By the time I had thought all these thoughts the elevator had reached the second floor and Helen stepped out. The doors closed. My life went on, in a vertical direction.

As soon as I plugged into my headset the bad calls began. It was as if the universe were punishing me for dreaming wild trampoline dreams for nights on end. First came three calls in a row of raspy low voices telling me *I'm watching you, Celia.* Next, a masturbator. My head felt too large and my hands were swollen, and wouldn't you know it, that's when, for the first time since the St. Francis Hotel debacle, the Sock Man decided it was time to call into the Resident Billing Office to clear the air with me.

"To think I loved you, Celia," he said.

The whole of that awful night came rushing back.

"I'm sorry," I said. "The truth is, I'm in love with someone else."

I tried dutifully to bring Drew's face into focus inside my head, but it wouldn't appear, and wouldn't appear, and then to my astonishment my mind's eye was looking straight into the specter of the waif-like British supermodel known as Twiggy, floating there, and I grew absorbed in a thought about how much this floating head of a British supermodel resembled my friend Joe from childhood. In the meantime the Sock Man was trying to hold the sobs in but it wasn't working. His sobs were leaking out wetly.

"Don't worry, Mr. Willy," I said. "You'll get over me, I promise, and you're going to find the right person one day."

"You're a very stupid girl," he said. "You don't know what you've given up. You'll never again know what it means to be loved in the way I loved you. I'm talking about true love, honey pie. Love! Love! Love! Love! Love! You'll never know love, honey, because you're a sad twisted person and your heart is tiny and rotted."

I said I guessed I already knew all those things about myself before he'd shared his opinions with me, and that in spite of my tiny black heart, I really did hope that he would find his true love one day. I don't think he took my words as sincere. He said many more unkind things before he was done. Maybe if we'd been in the same room together, instead of talking through a telephone wire, he would have thought better of me. As I took my sad leave of him, I would have kissed the top of his head, so vulnerable, and so worthy of sympathy. If I'd met him when I was older, after I'd become more tolerant of people's sexual urges, I might well have agreed to join him for a night or two of sock fetish fun, but at the time I wasn't ready for it. My imagination was cramped by inherited intolerant narrow notions about love and sex and life and death. I still had some growing up to do.

After I said my sad good-bye to the Sock Man I thought that

would surely be it in the drama department for the day, but it didn't happen that way. The next call came in. I said: "This is Celia, how can I help you?" At once a woman began to scream through my headset that her son was dead. As I listened to this woman's feral lamentations, and as I felt her delirious emotions sift in through my left ear, I began to think Mr. Willy had not been so bad after all. Then I transferred that screaming woman to the floor supervisor and I thought no more about much of anything.

I did have one good call that day, in the end. Just before the call queue was about to switch off, a voice came whispering into my ear. The voice sounded deep and wise, and gurgly, and familiar.

"This is Celia, how can I help you?" I said.

"I'm watching over you, Celia," the voice said.

The voice didn't say: "I'm watching you."

It said: "I'm watching *over* you."

I wanted it to be true. I wanted to believe that someone, preferably someone with my best interests at heart, was watching over me. I let myself wonder if it was the Crab Queen herself, calling in to tell me she was watching over me, and to assure me that all would be well, and that she was sending me her blessings—even if at the same time I knew there was no such creature as the Crab Queen, and that it was probably just Drew calling me again, from Chico, because he loved to mock me. But maybe it wasn't Drew. I allowed myself to end my speculations for the day on an upbeat note, and told myself that it really had been the Crab Queen. Just this once.

As I left the building I saw a man standing catty-corner across the street. I noticed him because he was looking back at me and frowning. Maybe he was the mystery caller who kept telling me he was watching me, and maybe he wasn't that guy, but his eyes were intense and more than a little hostile, and as I made my way toward the train station he kept pace with me from across the street. When I sped up, he sped up. When I slowed, he slowed. Who was this guy? Another unhappy customer? A Sock Man relative? A private eye, sent by Drew to tail me? The fabled serial farter? Whoever he was, half a block later he turned a corner and began to walk in a direction that didn't match my direction. And I said to myself, "Celia, Celia, Celia, you're making things up again," and I tripped on a crack in the sidewalk, and went on. I felt weighed down by dullness and cynicism. The walk to the station felt like one long trudge. It was a Friday night and the train was packed and steaming. We started off with the usual jerk backward and as always it made the passengers standing in the aisle lean forward, then stumble, then recover their footing. I found a seat by a window. The woman next to me was already asleep and slumping. I'd needed to climb over her to get to my seat. Across from the sleeping woman sat a man with a gift bag on his lap and he kept peeking into the bag and smiling to himself. A team of junior high school girls in uniform was making its way down the aisle. The girls squeezed by with their field hockey sticks raised and went upstairs to the single seats in the upper deck. The usual crowd of tired navy-suited men with their briefcases and their five-o'clock shadows settled into their seats, or hung onto straps and stood in the aisle, and because of my mood, all of those men looked like Blake Goodman, and as if they had a bone to pick with me. I closed my eyes. The usual hum of voices and random conversations kept flowing into my ear—*time to buy new sneakers be kind to her honey half price at the dollar store*—and then I heard some kind of bustle, and opened my eyes, and saw a big woman, head down, pushing her odious way past the people standing in the aisle and hanging on to straps, and she kept coming, struggling on, as if swimming upstream, until she reached the place where I was sitting and where there was still a vacant seat directly across from me. It was Mrs. Robert Brisket. I recognized her all at once. The woman whose son was addicted to phone porno. The sad tall willow tree of a woman. The woman whose lips I'd ripped some days ago. She was wearing the same stylish trench coat as the last time I'd seen her. She climbed over the man with a gift bag in his lap and the sleeping woman and sat down directly across from me and now we were each sitting by the window, face-to-face and knee to knee. Mrs. Brisket was the one traveling backward. She did not acknowledge me. I couldn't tell if she recognized me or not. She laughed a small laugh. Presumably she felt relieved and triumphant to have snagged one of the last seats in the car. I heard the Crab Queen scuttling sideways across the windows. The train cackled on mindlessly. *Love and death. Love and death.*

Was Mrs. Brisket here to confront me? I couldn't tell. Maybe she was about to plead her case with me again. I could be more kindhearted this time. I could help her get her phone back in service. Maybe I should have felt alarmed, but I didn't feel alarmed. I'd been in a car accident recently, and I'd been shot at, not to mention how I'd sliced a man gently open. My husband was off somewhere. My life was meaningless, probably. My mind was too full of these other worries for me to worry so much about Mrs. Brisket. We rode along, and rode along, until I began to feel certain she didn't recognize me after all. She had encountered me outside the context of the phone company office and I was therefore invisible to her. That's the way it is with service workers. We are blank faces unless we're encountered in our place of employment. Many years later, I would take a life drawing class at a community college, where I would learn all about the invisibility of service workers when they are encountered outside of their work functions. One day I ran into the model from my class in a Macy's department store, where naturally she was fully clothed, and for the life of me I couldn't place her. I'd been drawing her naked body for eight weeks by then, studying every inch of skin and curve of cheek, but I could not say how I knew her. I supposed the same sort of phenomenon was going on with Mrs. Brisket as we sat here together in this train. She wasn't able to recognize me outside of a phone company context. I just happened to be sitting across from her in a coincidental way. I decided not to reintroduce myself.

"Don't you hate trains?" Mrs. Brisket said. Maybe to me. I wasn't sure.

"The terrible swaying," she continued. "I hate it. I hate the need to breathe other people's air. I hate the killings. Is this your stop?"

The train was slowing. The Millbrae station was coming up.

"Not yet," I said.

The train glided into the station. Some people left. Other people flowed in. The train went on. Mrs. Brisket sat with both hands in her pockets. I still wasn't sure if she knew who I was. She probably knew. She was probably here for a reason. The uncertainty made me so uncomfortable that I decided to confront her and find out.

"What are you doing here, Mrs. Brisket?" I said. "What do you want?"

"What do I want?" she said.

She wailed a tiny, hideous wail. The sound she made was so disturbing that my mind filled up with helpless scurrying-ant thoughts. I was the same, brain-wise, as an ant on the kitchen floor, watching a dustpan and a whisk broom descend from on high. I thought about standing up, climbing over the sleeping woman and the man with the gift bag on his lap, and walking away from Mrs. Brisket. But the ant-thoughts were busy in my brain and they made it impossible for me to find a way to stand, or to move. Mrs. Brisket in the meantime had covered her face with her hands. Underneath the hands I could hear her saying: "God. God. God. God. God."

When she took her hands away, her face was red and ragged.

"I'm sorry," she said. "I don't know where I'm going. I don't know what to do. I'm in a dreadful muddle."

"That's all right," I said. "Everything is going to be all right."

"I need to give you something, Celia," she said.

Now that she had called me by name, I thought she'd probably followed me onto this train for a reason. I felt trapped in a tiny cramped space with a woman whose emotions seemed indelicate and unpredictable. She took a crumpled piece of paper out of a pocket in her trench coat and held it out. That piece of paper had been folded and bent in so many directions that it looked like a secret message, written by a child, to be passed in a classroom from one desk to the next.

"Take it," she said.

I took it.

"Do you want me to read what's written on this paper, Mrs. Brisket?" I said.

Mrs. Brisket nodded.

I unfolded the paper. It took some time to unfold it all the way.

I read the words.

DEAR KILLER—

That was it. The rest of the page was blank.

I made myself stare at those two words for a long time. It seemed likely that those words meant something important to Mrs. Brisket. Maybe she had begun to write something on the paper and she had found herself at a loss for words and had been forced to leave the rest of the paper empty. I tried to feel kind feelings toward her. I knew all about the feeling of having your intended words swallowed up by emptiness. Of finding yourself so full of sudden feeling that you're rendered speechless and trembling in the dark. I wanted to understand her. And so I gave that paper all the attention it deserved. I tried to respect the unwritten parts, and to read between the lines. A time came when there was nothing left to do but fold up the paper again and hand it back to Mrs. Brisket, and so I did. She put it back into her pocket and patted it. She didn't seem to require me to comment on what I'd read. She seemed to forget all about me. She was looking out the window. She was staring out, scanning for a glimpse of something.

"This is about where it happened," she said. "This is about where my son died. He stepped in front of a train and died. He called me before he died. He told me he loved me. The next call was from the coroner. When his father found the phone bill it was the last straw. He threw Bobby out. If you'd listened to me, Celia, then it never would have happened. My son would be alive. I thought you deserved to know."

She said the words dully. There was no emotion in her face. None in her voice. And I felt so dull. Dull-headed, I mean. Like a dull dead block of wood. The people all around us carried on with their crossword puzzles, and their dozing, and their everyday conversations. There we were, Mrs. Brisket and I, hurtling through space in a tin-can train. The strangeness of everyday life overwhelms me sometimes. The way I sat in a train every day, for instance. The way I consented to hurl myself forward through space in a metal casing that was, in its own way, as deadly as a bullet. Mrs. Brisket's face looked calm and sleepy. Tears were falling down her cheeks in two well-behaved streams. She was trying to weep discreetly. To keep her emotions in check. She didn't want to attract attention to herself or to make the people in this car with us think she was off her rocker.

"I keep thinking if you'd just listened to me, then it wouldn't have happened," she said. "That's what I keep telling myself. That's crazy, isn't it? Even I know it's crazy to blame you. Look at you. You're so young. You're barely more than a child. You're somebody's child."

The train was slowing down. I didn't feel responsible for her son's death, but I didn't feel absolved of it, either. I didn't know what to feel. We were coming to the Redwood City station.

I wanted to be kind.

"Next stop, Redwood City," a crackling voice announced.

"I'm in such a muddle," Mrs. Brisket said.

"Mrs. Brisket," I said. "I need to get off at this station."

"I'm nothing," she said. "I don't know where I'm going. I can't remember."

I couldn't just get up and walk away. I couldn't leave her here, alone, on this terrible train. I didn't feel responsible for her son, but I felt something, and I couldn't just leave her like this, weeping and alone and hurtling through space.

"How about this," I said. "Come off this train with me. We'll sit and talk somewhere. You can tell me all about your son."

I felt better instantly because I knew in my bones I had done the right thing. I had said the right words. Although Mrs. Brisket wasn't my friend, we were tied together in a terrible way. My obligation to her was fragile, but not nonexistent. Trying to be kind to her, in her hour of need, felt right to me.

The train was coming to a stop, and I stood up.

Mrs. Brisket's eyes followed me. If eyes are windows to the soul, then Mrs. Brisket's soul at that moment was a deep still pool that went on forever and the pool was filled with carnivorous fish. I needed to look away.

The train made its typical backward jerk before coming to rest, the way trains do, and the standing people all swayed and righted themselves.

"This is where I get off, Mrs. Brisket," I said. "Do you want to come with me?"

She didn't answer. I walked toward the exit doors. I stepped off the train.

Mrs. Brisket followed.

Mrs. Brisket followed me to my mother's Oldsmobile where I unlocked the passenger door for her and she got in. After I got behind the wheel I sat there awhile and wondered what to do. I had no perfect plan for how to help this sad lost woman, or any plan at all. Taking her to a public place, where she might break down and embarrass herself, felt cruel, and so I decided to take her home with me. The sun was close to setting and all was gray and formless. I liked to think I had helped Mrs. Brisket already. It hadn't felt right to leave her alone on the train. Now things felt so calm between us. All the striving, stress, and conflict had been resolved. Together we had reached a peaceful balance, where we would help each other forget all about the terrible things in our lives for a few minutes. Maybe we could do that for each other, woman-to-woman. The woman sitting next to me sighed in a peaceful way and then she inhaled, sharply, as if in pain, and I figured she had temporarily forgotten about the death of her son and then remembered it. In the meantime, we'd reached my little street, my little home. Mrs. Brisket followed me up the walk. I turned the key and the door opened.

I switched on the light.

"Come on in, Mrs. Brisket," I said.

Mrs. Brisket entered my house as if entering a shrine.

"What a lovely home," she said.

"Please have a seat," I said.

We were dancing a solemn dance, we two. We were performing politeness rituals together, as structured as a minuet. It's the way people behave after a great sadness has come into their lives. I felt as if I had been practicing those rituals all my life. I knew what to do, and what to say, and how to help. Mrs. Brisket sat down in my mother's favorite armchair. She'd instinctively chosen to sit in the seat most beloved by my mother. It felt significant, but I could not have told you why. She sat like a wretched person with her big coat wrapped tight around her body and her hands clutched to her thin sides. I switched on a lamp and it filled the room with a golden glow. My Drew liked low-watt bulbs because they were economical. I liked them because the light they made was warm and yellow. Low-watt bulbs were something Drew and I had always agreed on from the beginning.

"Can I get you something to drink?" I asked her.

"Oh, no, no thank you," she said. "But maybe an ashtray, if you don't mind me smoking in your house. I'm in need of a cigarette, I think."

I got an ashtray, and found a book of matches. I lit her cigarette for her and she thanked me. I lit one for myself, too. We smoked dazedly. It kept us from needing to think or speak for some few minutes. I was sitting on the couch across from my guest. Maybe it was the warm yellow light, or maybe it was simple exhaustion, but either way Mrs. Brisket began to relax. I could see it. She stopped clutching that big coat around herself. She took long contemplative drags. When the time came we both reached to stub out our cigarettes at the same time and our hands almost touched. Then Mrs. Brisket sat back contentedly and so did I. A few seconds later, Mrs. Brisket frowned and pulled something out from behind a cushion and held it up. It was a knitting needle, the size used for knitting baby booties and other fine things, and there were a dozen perfect rows of white-wool stitches hanging from the needle.

"My mother loved to knit and to sew," I said. "I'm always finding her unfinished projects around the house."

"She's passed, then?"

I nodded.

"Oh," Mrs. Brisket said.

She gave those white stitches a few reverential strokes with her fingertips and then she set them aside on the occasional table next to where she sat.

"Are you sure I can't get you something, Mrs. Brisket?" I said. "Something to drink?"

"Oh, no," she said. "Thank you, but no."

We sat together, not speaking, in my mother's favorite room. The room with the big bay window in front. My mother had always said the light coming in that window in the morning was perfect for handwork. I used to sit in that bay window seat and read when I was a child, while my mother did her work. Most of the books I remembered from that time were still in the bookcases on either side of that window, and as Mrs. Brisket and I sat there with nothing to say, I looked those books over, reading the titles. Here was my mother's beloved, tattered copy of *The Singer Sewing Book*. Next to it was my beloved *F* volume of the *Encyclopædia Britannica*. A salesman had come to the door one afternoon and left that *F* volume with my mother as a sample, and he'd never followed up with the rest of the alphabet. Maybe he'd found a better job. It was an era when door-to-door salesmen were about to become extinct and maybe that's what happened to him. Whatever the truth of the matter, I'd never missed the other books of the encyclopedia because the *F* volume was full of wonders, like "Flags of the World" and "Frogs." Next to the encyclopedia was a book called *The Sea*. It had been my all-time-favorite book as a child. Inside was an illustration of burly fishermen hurling chum over the side of their little boat, a practice that had naturally attracted the attention of all the sharks in the sea, setting them off on a feeding frenzy so frenzied that those sharks were chomping on each other and the sea was pink and bloody. Every time I went in the ocean I would think of that book and of that picture. I began to grow wary of shadows on water, even in swimming pools. Even more life-affecting than the chum illustration was the photograph of long-legged crabs in that book, and even more life-affecting than the crabs was the stonefish. The stonefish looked like a stone, and stepping on it meant instant death. It didn't matter that the stonefish was native to Australian waters because the waters were all connected, and not just the waters, either—everything was connected. Everything. Love and death. Joy and grief. All these random thoughts about old times swirled about in my head and made me feel peaceful. Mrs. Brisket patted the upholstery. Then she touched her lips and looked all around.

"It's so nice to sit here, in this cozy home," Mrs. Brisket said. "It's so nice to sit in this cozy armchair. I don't think I've ever felt so cozy in all my life."

"You're very welcome, Mrs. Brisket," I said. "I'm glad you feel at home. This was my mother's favorite room."

Out the bay window I saw the shadows of cars coming down the street and pulling into driveways.

"Daddy!" a child shouted.

Mrs. Brisket and I sat in the glow of the yellow lamp.

"He was a good kid," Mrs. Brisket said. "Do you have children, Celia? No, of course you don't, you're just a baby, like my son—"

She came urgently over to where I was sitting on the couch and sat down next to me and took my hand in hers. I squeezed her hand warmly. My squeeze was meant to let her know she could hold my hand just as long as she wanted. I think, in those moments, she needed to touch another living person. It helped her keep breathing.

"Tell me about your boy," I said.

"Let me tell you about my boy," she said.

Her face was joyous. She began to tell me about her boy from the beginning. Here is a mother, telling me about the perfection of her newborn child, her son, so small and so new. The mother rejoices in that small perfect boy. Perfect. Yes. From the first day. A gentle boy. Loves his mom. When the boy is two he falls and cuts his lip open. The mother learns the terrible lesson every mother must learn, that she doesn't have the power to keep her child always safe. All this time, as Mrs. Brisket told me about her boy, the world around us grew smaller and smaller, until it was just us two. I'd felt that feeling before, of all the world and its glories collapsing down and down until the world was no more than just two people, sharing something sacred. I felt honored, and sad. So many other feelings were swirling around in my body. There are not many events in life like the naked sadness of listening to a mother as she tells you stories, all in the past tense, about her dead child. By this time in her story about her son Mrs. Brisket was holding my hand so tightly. The feelings coming out of her were enormous. She was squeezing my hand so completely that her nails dug into the skin and I didn't care. I could be strong. I could be here for her. I could take it. With my free hand I touched her shoulder. It was barely a touch, but it broke something open in her. She wrapped both her arms around me and laid her head down on my chest like a child trying to snuggle in closer to its mother, and she began to cry in the way a brokenhearted child will cry, in endless agonizing sobs. I didn't pull away. I patted her on the back, stupidly. All this time I'd been thinking I knew everything there was to know about love and death. Now that I was sitting here, with a grieving mother in my arms, I knew that every thought I'd ever thought before about love and death had been a childish thought, as empty of any true understanding as an old pickle jar. I didn't know the first thing about love and death. I'd been playacting all along. I didn't know what to say or do and so I just kept patting her on the back. Then I began to hum a little hum. Maybe Mrs. Brisket took some solace from the sound. Her sobbing softened, until the sounds she was making stretched into some other kind of sound, more like a moan, or a bleat, or a surrender. I felt her relax into me. She'd cried herself out for the time being. Here she rested. I held her as closely as I could, until we were breathing in time together, heartbeat to heartbeat. We stayed that way for a long time, holding on to each other as if our lives depended on it, and then she adjusted herself in my arms, as if trying to adjust herself to a new reality, and that is about when I felt the unmistakable steel-hard shape of a gun, nestled there between our nested bodies.

All was still. All was dreadfully, dreadfully still.

"Are you about to shoot me, Mrs. Brisket?" I said.

I would never know her answer to this question because the front door opened with a bang and here was Drew, come home in time to catch me in a clenched embrace with a stranger, and my dumb husband rushed forward, looming, enraged—*What the hell, Celia!*—and Mrs. Brisket—startled, terrified, grief-addled—who can say what she was feeling?—leapt up—

The roar of a gun—

And then?

We stood there, Mrs. Brisket and I, until there was no doubt about it. The man at our feet was dead. You could tell he was dead by the look on his face. The bewilderment. The gore. I looked at the dead man on the floor. I looked at Mrs. Brisket. Mrs. Brisket was doing the same sort of looking, from me to the dead man and back to me—how confounding it seemed to us both, to find ourselves here, together, at this strange new juncture, with a dead man at our feet!—and Mrs. Brisket, unable to contain her astonishment any longer, raised the gun to her broken heart and shot once more.

And maybe I thought: "Celia, you need to sit down."

I can't remember what I thought.

I do remember I sat down. I sat down in my mother's favorite armchair. I didn't look over there. I didn't pick up the phone. I didn't inform the relevant authorities that two people had just died in my house, of unnatural causes. I kept hoping someone else would do the informing. I didn't want to look over there. Maybe I was thinking that if I waited here long enough, hoping against hope, then someone would surely come in through my front door and tell me it was all a terrible dream. They would come over to where I sat, open-mouthed and barely breathing, and take pity on me, and say: "Don't worry, Celia. Everything is going to be all right." That's all I wanted. To have someone, anyone at all, come up to me and say: "Don't worry, Celia. Everything is going to be all right." They'd probably need to say it a second time before I'd believe it. It didn't happen. I still didn't look over there. I tried to think optimistically, but nobody came. Time began to behave so strangely. Wait and see. Times like these come for us all. The particulars will be different, but times like these will surely come for you, and when they do, there will be no pulse in the world. No heartbeat. Seconds and minutes won't behave. One moment you'll be living through staccato time where everything feels sharp and bright and fast, and the next you'll be stuck in geologic time and you'll have turned to stone. I'm trying to explain why I sat there. Why

I didn't pick up the phone. Why I didn't look over there. Dawn seeped in, surprising me. I didn't expect it. I watched the light in the room turn gray and cold, and still I didn't look over there, and still I sat, and still I felt as if no time had passed at all, and I was nothing.

TEN

THE CONFESSION

For the rest of my life I'd belong to a sad, strange club of people who had survived a shooting. It used to be quite an exclusive club, but over the years our numbers would grow, and grow some more, and sometimes we would come together and share our stories, and whenever I shared my story—the story I'm about to relate to you now, about what happened to me and how my life changed forever after I witnessed the death by murder of my husband, and the death by suicide of my husband's killer—a random man in our survivor-circle would inevitably leap up and shout: "You lie! It could never have happened that way! You would have been taken away from the scene at once! Fingerprint powder is *black*!"—and the women in the circle would shush this loudmouth and tell him to back off already, and then these women would tell me I should never let anyone, least of all a man, try to talk me out of my truth—and since what I'm about to tell you is my truth, I will go on.

Once more the sound of gunshots in the night had been, to the neighbors, as silent as the void. It wasn't until the next morning that a neighbor called the police. Not because they'd heard gunshots. Not because they harbored the slightest suspicion that the cops would find a couple of dead people in the house across the way. No. They called the cops because there was a Ford Pinto parked crazily, half up on the curb and half in the street and with the driver's-side door wide open, and there was a dead deer tied to the roof of that car, and the deer was beginning to attract the attention of blowflies and crows. Its long black tongue was sticking out. It was scaring the children. The neighborhood dogs kept barking and yapping and trying to leap up and take a bite out of the dead animal's flanks. Those dogs were causing quite a ruckus. At this point the neighborhood gossip was all about the Ford Pinto with a dead deer on top. No one was talking about the way my husband had come flying out of that Pinto the night before, so eager to catch me in a slutty act that he left his car door wide open and ran up to the house and burst through the front door and rushed headlong toward his fate. I would never know whether Drew had come home to kiss and make up with me, or if he'd come home certain he was about to catch me red-handed in the act of some cheap betrayal. Either way, what he'd seen through that big bay window was his wife in the arms of somebody who wasn't him, confirming all his worst fears about me, and so he'd rushed in. The way fools do.

The first officer to arrive at the scene thought he was there to ring the doorbell and ask the man of the house to do the right thing by that deer. As he came up the walk, his eyes narrowed because he had just spied a waxy hand, suspiciously still, through the front door, which was ajar. He pushed the door open. Moving that arm. Disrupting the crime scene. He'd get a reprimand for that, later. In the meantime, here I was, sitting in my mother's favorite armchair with my hands in my lap and my ankles demurely crossed. I was so still. I'd been turned to granite cliff by all those long and lonely hours of my night vigil. I watched the officer check the pulses of the two dead bodies over there. After finding their pulses absent, the officer stood up and crossed himself.

He was on his walkie-talkie, calling for backup, when his eyes slid over to my side of the room.

"What the heck are you doing over there?" he said.

"I live here," I said.

"Hands in the air where I can see them!" he said.

And then I was on the floor with a knee in my back, and my hands cuffed behind.

It was one of those TV years when police procedurals became all the rage. CBS, NBC, ABC—it didn't matter where you flipped the dial, because wherever you landed, there the cops would be, busy with their cop affairs. All the cops coming in through the door in the next few minutes had clearly watched the same shows I had watched. They were all doing exactly the things that TV cops did, snapping Polaroids and taping up police tape to mark the scene of the crime and so on.

One of them helped me up from the floor and sat me gently back in my mother's favorite armchair.

"A detective will be with you soon, ma'am," he said, and went away.

Two solemn men came in and zipped the bodies into long white bags and took them away.

By this time there was a fine powder, white as new snow, scattered all over the place. Forensics experts had left white fingerprint powder everywhere, messily, after dusting for fingerprints. I couldn't get over the way all the things they were doing felt uncannily familiar to me, from the shows. The words they spoke back-and-forth sounded like a TV script. From the vantage point of where I sat it felt like I was watching them on a jumbo TV screen. But wait a minute. How likely is it that those cops would have left me sitting there in my mother's favorite armchair while they went about their business? How likely is it that I felt as if I were watching those detectives on a jumbo

TV screen, when large-screen television technology was still decades away? How likely is it that I'd be sitting there full of nostalgic thoughts about police procedurals from the seventies on the morning after I'd witnessed a crazed gunwoman shoot my husband dead at close range? Wouldn't I have been thinking about my Drew and how he was dead and so on? Is fingerprint powder black? Whenever I ask myself these bald questions, I begin to think those red-faced buffoons in my survivor circles were right all along. Oh yes, my dears. It could be that the so-called facts I'm relating to you from the here-and-now are no more than shattered fragments pieced together by a mind that was barely functioning at the time. In fact it would not surprise me in the least if nearly all of the so-called memories I'm relating to you, from the here-and-now, are nothing but scraps of stories borrowed from late-night reruns of those same cop shows from the seventies that I've watched over the years. No wonder my so-called memories of the day track so closely with TV crime. They might be one and the same. At any rate, just then a plainclothes detective pulled a chair up next to mine and sat in it. He leaned forward, with his elbows on his knees. His suit jacket smelled of tobacco. I wanted to ask him for a smoke, but I thought he might form a negative opinion about me and so I didn't. Tobacco products of all kinds were falling from favor in those days. Celebrities still smoked, but they didn't inhale. Clever ashtrays abounded in both public and private spaces but in a few years they'd be gone forever.

"Sorry to keep you waiting, Mrs. Dent," he said. "Is there anything I can do to make you more comfortable, while we wrap up here?"

He could see for himself that my face and clothes were spattered with blood and bits of viscera. I'd already told him the blood on my face was itching. He'd already told me I couldn't wash it off just yet because the blood might be evidence for all he knew. My hands were cuffed behind my back. I couldn't scratch what itched. Under the circumstances, I had to wonder why he was asking about my comfort.

"I'm fine," I said.

"May I call you Celia?" he said.

"All right," I said.

"Very well, then, Celia," he said.

"And what may I call you?" I said.

"Detective Pritzker," he said.

Detective Pritzker took a little notepad and a stub of a pencil out from his jacket pocket.

"What was the nature of your relationship with Mrs. Robert Brisket?" he said.

His question was a puzzler. I didn't know how I'd ever explain to this earnest detective that it had been my idea to invite the crazed gunwoman Mrs. Brisket into my home. I wasn't sure how to break it to him that I'd also spent some number of minutes consoling the grief-filled gunwoman in my arms just before she leapt up and shot my Drew in the throat. Even in my sleep-deprived, blood-spattered state, I was thinking it might not be in my best interest to tell him about the coldhearted decision I'd made some days ago to rip Mrs. Brisket's lips, a thing I'd done on a whim, that had, in turn, caused a tragic chain of consequences that led to the death of Mrs. Brisket's only son, and the death of Drew, and the death of Mrs. Brisket herself. I decided to spare Detective Pritzker all these complicated details. But I may have pondered these things too long, or given Detective Pritzker the impression I was hiding something, because he stood abruptly and said, "If that's how you want it, ma'am, then we'll finish our little talk down at the station." Then he led me by the elbow—the way men typically led women, back then, whether those women were handcuffed or not—and into a waiting patrol car out front. A neighbor or two had gathered in the street. People watched curiously as Detective Pritzker bundled me into the back seat of his car and drove off. When we got to the station, he led me into a windowless room and left me there. I never saw him again. The door opened, and two men wearing identical neckties came into the room and seated themselves across from me at the table. They introduced themselves as "Parker" and "Mitchell." The cop shows in that era were all known by the last names of their cop-hero protagonists—Kojak. Cannon. Banyon. Hawkins. Griff. I figured Parker and Mitchell had been influenced by the trend.

"You're a cold one, aren't you, Mrs. Dent?" Mitchell said.

"She's a cold one, isn't she?" Parker said.

"Am I a suspect?" I said hysterically. "Are you suspecting me?"

"What makes you think you're a suspect?" Parker said.

From my own viewing habits of prime-time police procedurals, I knew what to say next.

"I want my phone call," I said.

I called Randall Smiley.

"Oh, sweetheart, I know just the man," Randall said.

Randall Smiley's lawyer's name was Tony Petrocelli, and he'd just successfully steered Randall through the paperwork and consequences that typically come along after a man finds himself hiding under his married lover's bed when her husband comes bursting into the bedroom and shoots her dead. It was my bad luck that Mr. Petrocelli was a square-dance aficionado. He was busy dancing that weekend at "The Golden State Round Up" in Bakersfield, over four hours away. Randall had a heck of a time tracking him down. To his credit, he kept trying, and to Mr. Petrocelli's credit, he came as soon as he could, without even taking time to change out of his fringed shirt and cowboy boots.

In the meantime, Parker and Mitchell kept asking me questions without my lawyer present. I had trouble focusing. I kept rolling Mitchell's words around in my head. You're a cold one. You're a *cold* one. I checked to see if I was crying, and I wasn't. I decided Mitchell was probably right. I was probably a cold one. *You're* definitely *a cold one*, said Drew's voice, next to my ear. *And you're disgusting. I don't understand you at all. Your husband just died and you can't even cry. There is something wrong with you, Celia. I guess you're just a killer.*

Hearing Drew's voice so close to my ear made me flinch.

Parker saw it.

"What is it, Mrs. Dent?" he said eagerly. "Is there anything you want to tell us? It will go easier on you if you tell us."

I nearly "shushed" Parker, because too many voices were talking to me at the same time.

You killed me, Drew's voice was saying in my left ear.

Tell them you don't know anything, the Crab Queen was saying in my right ear.

"I don't know anything," I said.

"Was the late Mrs. Brisket your clandestine lover?" Mitchell said.

"I don't know," I said.

"Was Mrs. Brisket your late husband's clandestine lover?" Mitchell said.

I guessed by this line of questioning that Mitchell was developing a "lover's tryst gone awry" theory of the case. I didn't blame Mitchell for taking that leap. It's only natural for men of the law to go straight to the "lover's tryst gone awry" theory of the case whenever three adults are mixed up in a crime that ends in violent death.

"I don't know," I said.

"You don't know much, Mrs. Dent," Mitchell said.

Parker changed the subject. He wanted to know about the bullet they'd found buried in my kitchen wall. The kitchen-wall bullet didn't fit with my statement.

"Did you forget to tell us something, Mrs. Dent?" he said. "Would you care to revise your statement? Maybe you can explain to us what that bullet was doing in your kitchen wall?"

I was reluctant to explain how the bullet got there. Any explanation worth its salt would lead me to reveal that Drew had fired a warning salvo at me after I'd come home late from a debauched night of revelry that included an episode of me slicing a well-tailored bounder open like a hot cross bun. I didn't want to get into it with Parker, especially when I knew full well the bullet in the kitchen wall was a red herring.

In walked Mr. Petrocelli and everything changed. The air, the light, the smell. I could tell Mr. Petrocelli was the genuine article, not just because of his stylish fringed cowboy wear but also because he sported muttonchop whiskers.

"Are these cuffs absolutely necessary, gentlemen?" Mr. Petrocelli said. "This slip of a girl weighs less than my arm!"

I was uncuffed. Mr. Petrocelli sat down next to me. Parker lost interest in the mystery bullet and began to ask me instead why I'd sat there all night in a room with two dead people instead of doing what anyone else would have done, which was to pick up the gosh-darn telephone and report the crime. "We might have been able to save your husband's life if you'd acted rationally," he kept saying. Was Parker right? Could I have saved my Drew with a phone call? I thought back on the way my husband had looked at me just after Mrs. Brisket fired her first volley. In my memory Drew's eyes looked instantly dead. But what did I know? Had I ever seen a live person shot dead before? I had not.

I began to doubt everything, everything.

"I don't think you could have saved him," I said.

I might have sounded uncertain, or uneasy, or petulant, or guilty, though, because my mutton-chopped lawyer interjected.

"Have you ever seen someone murder the love of your life right in front of you?" Mr. Petrocelli said. He said it quietly. From the shows, I would have expected a more demonstrative delivery, accompanied by a pounded fist to the table. But Mr. Petrocelli had his own methods.

"Can you honestly be certain, gentlemen, that you wouldn't have sat there, in shock, hoping against hope that someone was about to come in through the door and tell you it was all a terrible dream? If you have never once watched the love of your life mowed down in cold blood, then please, I beg of you, don't be so quick to judge."

Mr. Petrocelli looked down at his folded hands. So did we all look down at our own folded hands.

A little man wearing suspenders opened the door and stepped in and we all looked up.

The man whispered in Mitchell's ear. He handed Mitchell a piece of notepaper.

He went away.

Mitchell read the note.

He looked at me significantly.

"Did your late husband work at the phone company, Mrs. Dent?" he said.

"What?" I said.

"What did your late husband do for a living, Mrs. Dent?" Mitchell said.

"My late husband was an unemployed scrub tech," I said.

"Detective Mitchell, might I ask what the significance of that note in your hand might be?" Mr. Petrocelli said.

"It seems the late Mrs. Brisket has left behind a full confession," Mitchell said. "It seems she left home last night with the premeditated intention to kill someone dead before the night was through."

Mitchell seemed disappointed by this new evidence. His tone was bitter. He'd been on the verge of throwing me in the clinker for my random crimes and I wouldn't have blamed him for it, because I'd recently left a trail of mayhem and death in my wake without even trying.

"Apparently Mr. Brisket discovered his wife's confession when he was getting dressed to come down to the station," Mitchell continued. "It seems Mrs. Brisket rolled her confession up and stuck it in her husband's left dress shoe at some point before she went out on her murder spree."

"What?" Parker said.

"I said she rolled it up and put it in her husband's left shoe, Parker," Mitchell said. "So he'd find it just as soon as he stuck a toe in."

"Lemme see that," Parker said.

Parker took the note from Mitchell, and I heard him mutter-read: I have made up my mind to end the life of a phone company employee tonight. Don't cry for me, Robert. Justice must be served.

"Needless to say, this is good news for you, Mrs. Dent," Mitchell said. "Because frankly, I find you suspicious."

"What did the phone company ever do to that woman?" Parker said. "Honestly, Mitchell. Who hates the phone company?"

I could have told Parker that plenty of people hate the phone company, especially just after their lips get ripped. I could have additionally told him that the mystery phone company employee in the room the night before had been me, not my Drew. My soul was in a turmoil about the sudden discovery of a left-behind confession penned by Mrs. Brisket. I didn't want to believe there was paper-proof that Mrs. Brisket had planned to kill me all along. I decided not to believe it. I wouldn't believe it! She had forgiven me in the end. I was sure of it. How else to explain the way she'd cried into my bosom while I patted her consolingly? How else to explain the second letter she had written, that two-word note, so full of portent and feeling, that she'd handed to me on the train before we'd gone home together, to smoke, and to cry, and to find solace in each other's arms?

DEAR KILLER, she'd written.

Because I'd been "dear" to her.

She should have shot you dead, Drew's voice said next to my ear. *It's what you deserved.*

"Your statement, Mrs. Dent, is that your late husband was *not* a phone company employee?" Mitchell said.

I shook my head.

"Did your husband ever work at the phone company?"

I shook my head.

I was in a funky muddle. I was at the breaking point. My sins and crimes were rising up in my brain like spiteful specters, accusing me. For the sake of my soul, I needed to tell Mitchell and Parker the whole story. These two brave detectives deserved to know that *I* was the evil phone company employee upon whom Mrs. Brisket had planned to heap her vigilante justice, and that I'd deserved it, for all the death and destruction I'd caused. Poor Mrs. Brisket! Poor Bobby Brisket! Poor Drew! Poor Blake Goodman! Poor Sock Man! Poor Mother! Poor Barbies!—but before I could spill the beans Mr. Petrocelli sensed my overwhelming compulsion to set the record straight, and, good lawyer that he was, he interrupted me.

"Gentlemen," he said. "Who can say why Mrs. Brisket mistook my client's husband for a phone company employee? Who can say what led this woman's troubled mind to the doorstep of my client? Who can say why she pulled the trigger, not once, but twice?"

I'm *the one*, I tried to say—I'm *the one who can set the record straight*—but Mr. Petrocelli had his hand on my shoulder by then. He was squeezing it with vigor. His message was being transmitted by the pain shooting up from my shoulder, from his squeezes. *Now is not the time to tell your story*, his squeezes said.

"We'll never know the answers to these questions," Mr. Petrocelli said. "What we do know is that the time has come for you to let this poor girl go home to grieve in peace!"

Thanks to Mr. Petrocelli's timely squeezes, I remained silent. As was my right. Remaining silent had been my right ever since Ernesto Miranda's landmark case in 1966. Think of it. One man, named Ernesto, single-handedly altered the dialogue in every climactic scene in every true-crime show and police procedural to come, forevermore, and what's more, thanks to Ernesto, I was walking away a free woman, but with a soul still burdened by my unconfessed crimes.

We all stood up. The men shook hands all around.

Mr. Petrocelli walked out with me. We may have exchanged some friendly chitchat but I don't remember. The only voice I remember hearing, as I stepped out of the station and into the sun—squinting, upended, newly widowed—was Drew's voice, close to my ear.

Where can you go? the voice said.

Drew's voice hadn't yet caught up with the facts.

I was nineteen years old.

It was just past four o'clock, on a Saturday afternoon.

ELEVEN

LOVE AND LIFE

Mr. Petrocelli brought me home from the police station but after he dropped me off and drove away I didn't go inside the house. I didn't want to. Not even to wash the blood and bits of viscera from my skin. I was afraid to go in there and face the reverberant empty silence of that house. I'd hear the echoes of gunshots. I'd hear the voice of Drew. Instead of going inside, I got into my mother's Oldsmobile and went for a drive. I drove east, then south. I had no particular destination in mind. I just needed to move. The first time I stopped for gas, I went straight into the ladies' room and washed my face. Then I changed my clothes. Thanks to my skill with procrastination, I had a big pile of dirty laundry in the trunk, and plenty of clothes to choose from, left there by me from the day when delinquents had broken into my car some lifetimes ago. Those clothes might have been in need of a launder back when I'd been a billing operator, but now my circumstances had changed and they didn't seem so dirty. That night I slept in my mother's Oldsmobile. After that I lost track of the days. I kept following the open road. I learned you can sleep in a car unmolested by cops if you choose your space wisely and move to a new space each night. I didn't want to go back to work ever again. I didn't want to go home. The thought of walking through the front door and stepping over a big bloodstain on the carpet to get anywhere else in the house gave me such bad shakes that I'd need to lie down flat and wait for the nausea to pass, wherever I might be. At the gas station. At the dollar store. People would crowd around. They'd lean over me and shout: "Miss! Miss!" and I'd try to assure them that I was in no danger of swallowing my tongue or having a stroke. "I'm all right, really," I'd say. "It's just the shakes. I'll be out of your way in just a minute," and then they'd frown and mutter as if I'd disappointed them, and one of them would probably say, "Hey, aren't you the one who's in all the papers?" and I would act as if I'd just forgotten how to speak until they went away. I ate from cans. I hung out in libraries, reading newspapers on sticks. I was front-page news. The papers got a lot of details wrong. Mrs. Brisket never took me hostage, for instance. People just wrote it that way. It made more sense than the truth. I drove places. I was literally in the driver's seat. It amazed me, the way I could drive in any direction I pleased. To Mexico, or Canada, or all the way to New York City, or straight into the Pacific Ocean. Once before, I'd sat behind the wheel of my mother's Oldsmobile and thought these thoughts, but then the additional thought of Drew, waiting at home for me, had stopped me in my tracks. Now I was tetherless. I was a migratory bird. I'd drive all day until I stopped and then there I'd be, in Fresno or Weed, or Barstow. All of this driving felt purposeful even though it was aimless.

Sometimes I would scold myself for all the things I wasn't doing that needed to get done. "Celia, you have got to go home and take care of that dead deer carcass in your front yard!" I'd say to myself. Or: "Celia! Come on! You need to plan a funeral for your husband and bury him, gosh darn it. Rally yourself!" But as soon as I reminded myself of the things I was supposed to be doing, I'd sink into a listless funk and drive in a new direction.

One night as I was parked and sleeping in the back seat in a lot behind a furniture warehouse in Lancaster, a beautiful dream came to me. The dream was gone in an instant and I woke up with a flashlight shining in my eyes. The dream-feeling remained. I felt beatific. I felt absolved. I wanted the light in my eyes to go away. A knuckled rap on the back window came and when I rolled down the window I saw that the cops had found me. Or: just one cop, actually, making his nightly rounds to search out hidden miscreants and vagabonds. He said, "Out of the car!"—and I complied. When I had no trouble walking a straight line for him, he gave me a fix-it ticket for the broken window in front that I'd patched up with cardboard and electrician's tape, so long ago, and then he told me to move on because I was sleeping on private property. I got back in the car. I drove out of the lot at a sober speed. I'd fallen into one of those half-dazed, half-wide-awake states of mind that come to you just after you're awakened abruptly in the middle of the night from a revelatory dream, when everything seems so clear and purposeful, and simple, and as I pulled onto the road a new voice came into my head, and the voice said: *It's time to rescue that dog.*

It was a six-hour drive from Lancaster to Belmont, home of the valiant Doggo. For a long time I'd been thinking Blake Goodman was probably the kind of man who'd send his dog off to the pound in retribution for that bite to his leg, even if the dog's pedigree stretched all the way back to Horand von Grafrath, and I'd felt bad for leaving that dog behind enemy lines, so to speak. I stopped four times on the way to Belmont, twice for gas, once to check a tire, and once to buy myself a breakfast with extra bacon at a diner in Paso Robles. I got to Belmont about noon. I hadn't been back to that town since the night I'd walked home along El Camino Real with a knife in my boot, after a wild evening of winks and drinks, and socks, and rough fondlings, and a swift slice to a man's paunch, and a dog's meaty chomp to his master's leg. That was the night Drew shot a bullet six inches from my head. If he'd gone straight for the kill shot then he could have saved himself from his deadly encounter with Mrs. Brisket, not so many days later, but it was not to be.

Now that I was back in Belmont, I'd hit a snag. So much had happened in the world since the night the valiant Doggo had defended me—the death of Bobby Brisket—the death of Drew—the death of Mrs. Brisket—the resignation of a U.S. president—the creation of an independent Guinea-Bissau—that everything looked different to me, and I could not find my way. I drove in circles for an hour only to find myself back where I'd started, in front of the Belmont train station.

I tried a new tactic. I parked my mother's Oldsmobile in front of the station and got out. I closed my eyes and waited for my proprioceptive intuitions to kick in. Sometimes you need the patience of a water witcher to know which way to turn. My feet, in this case, were going to be the metaphorical forked stick. I was stuck until I visualized that noble dog biting into the meaty part of his master's calf. My feet began to move. They'd found the path. Minutes later I was standing at the head of a long driveway lined with giant oleander bushes. At the other end I could see the circular roundabout where Blake Goodman had parked his little Porsche, just before he'd led me by the hand up those big stone steps. Here was the same white house, with the same Corinthian columns in front. By day that house looked gray and a little shabby, and the scene before me was full of unexpected bustle. I'd imagined a still and empty house with a lone dog inside it, patiently waiting for me to rescue him. Instead here was this man riding back and forth across the lush lawn, mowing it. Other men were busy on ladders by the front door. There was a van parked in the circular roundabout in front of the house, with the words A.B. PIEPERS & SONS—YOUR HOME SECURITY EXPERTS painted on its side. My plan had been to find a handy brick and to break a window with it and to find the "dog room" and stealthily whisk Doggo away to freedom. I'd thought my plan was foolproof. My foolproof plan was in tatters.

A woman stepped out from behind one of the giant oleander bushes, not a dozen feet away.

"You must be the new dog-walker," the woman said.

"Hello," I said.

"You don't look like a Maria," she said.

"It was my grandmother's name," I said.

This was true.

"You must be Lavinia Goodman," I said next.

It was an educated guess that turned out to be right.

Lavinia pulled off one of her garden gloves and we shook hands.

"Call me Lavinia," she said. "Come meet Ace! I'm so glad you're here, Maria. Ever since the break-in, the dog has been highly agitated. He bit my husband!"

I followed Lavinia down the long driveway. From the back, she looked the perfect picture of one of those women I'd always admired from a distance and foolishly hoped I'd grow up to be: coiffed, pert, chipper. The man sitting atop the lawn mower waved to us as we passed, and then rode on. We walked by the men on ladders. Then I was inside this house again. The floor was pristine. The space smelled like fresh mint.

"Sorry for the mess," Lavinia said. "What a hubbub. Men have been here all morning installing a security system. You wouldn't believe what my husband and I have been through lately. Last month four men broke into the house. They stole my jewelry. They stabbed my husband. They left him for dead."

"Golly," I said. "Is he okay?"

"It's a miracle but he's okay," Lavinia said. "He keeps saying, 'Thank God you were away that night, Lavinia, because I hate to think what those men would have done to you!'"

"Too bad about your jewelry," I said.

I guessed Blake had hidden that jewelry, to bolster his story about where he'd come by the slash in his midsection. Maybe he'd given the jewelry away to a girlfriend or two. I could imagine it.

"That's what homeowner's insurance is for," Lavinia said.

"Are those cameras filming us?" I said.

"Not yet," she said. "Mr. Piepers says the system will be up and running by seven o'clock tonight. Cameras. Alarms. The whole shebang. After seven o'clock tonight, you'd have a better chance of breaking out of Alcatraz than breaking into this house."

"Amazing," I said.

"Oh, well," Lavinia said. "Don't you think break-ins are like lightning, though? I think break-ins are like lightning. They never strike the same house twice. I keep telling Blake we're wasting our money installing a security system when lightning will never strike here again. Don't you agree? That break-ins are like lightning?"

"I haven't thought about it," I said.

"You should think about it," Lavinia said. "We should all think about it. Blake says a man's home is his castle and his castle has been breached."

"I've heard that before," I said.

"It's one of those things men say," Lavinia said. "Blake wants us to move to Marin. I say the guys who attacked him will never come back here. They wouldn't dare. On the other hand, properties in Marin are a bargain these days. Blake might talk me into it. Thank God I was at my sister's bachelorette party in Cabo— Here we are! Ace! Come meet your new little dog-walker!"

That dog gave me a doleful look, and I didn't blame him.

Then he walked over to me and licked my hand, and we were friends.

"You have a way with dogs," Lavinia said.

I thought it best to keep looking as if I had a way with dogs.

Since we were in the fabled "dog room," there was a leash hanging from a hook on the wall. I took the leash down with an authoritative flourish. I snapped it expertly onto Doggo's collar.

"I'll be taking Ace for a good long walk today," I said. "It helps the bond. The first walk needs to be a good long walk. Don't expect us back before this evening."

"In that case, I might not be home when you get back," Lavinia said. "Blake might be here, but he works late sometimes. Here's a key to the house. If you come back after seven p.m., you'll need to disable the new security system. There's a keypad by the front door. I'll show you on our way out. The passcode is *G, O, O, D, M, A, N.*"

She handed me a house key.

"It spells *Goodman,*" Lavinia said. "That's our name."

She looked at me so sweetly that I wanted to spill the beans and tell her she was married to a bounder. But maybe she wasn't ready to hear it. Or maybe she knew it already. We're each on our own path in this life and no one can walk it for us.

"Very good," I said.

On the way out Lavinia showed me the little keypad by the door. She made me practice punching in the passcode. Together we made our way back down the long driveway until we came to the oleander bush where Lavinia had been busy digging up the dandelions before I'd showed up. This leisurely stroll down the driveway with Doggo prancing by my side and Lavinia talking on about real estate felt like the most perilous few minutes of the entire caper. I kept expecting Maria the dogwalker to pop into view at the other end of the drive and come toward us with a bounce in her step and an expectant look on her face, and that would be the end of me. But it didn't happen.

Just before we parted ways, I told Lavinia I'd be exercising the dog with vigor.

"I'll be picking up the pace from now on," I said. "It's always good to jog a dog."

"Wonderful," Lavinia said.

I wanted to tell Lavinia to take good care of herself, and to never settle for less than she deserved. But she had already gone back to her dandelions. And I doubted she would listen to advice from a dog-walker. So Doggo and I broke into a run. We ran all the way to our getaway car, and then the two of us were driving off together, as free as the wind, and as fast as we could go without breaking any more traffic laws than necessary.

"Where to, my fine doggo?" I said, and that dog looked so much like a dog who had never once run along a beach that I decided to take him there.

I remember the drive over the hills that day with exceptional clarity. The sky was the color of a Mexican opal and the sun had burnished the clouds to a high polish. After I came to the coast road I turned south, and when we got to the San Gregorio General Store, the only store along that stretch, I stopped and bought a bag of dog chow and two big bowls. Before we got back in the car I gave Doggo a feast of kibble and water and he lapped them both right up and we went on our way. A few miles later I parked by the side of the road and Doggo and I ran straight down to the sand. There was nobody on that stretch of beach and that was not so surprising because the water along that part of the coast is frigid-cold. The only sign of human life was a line of surfers, far out to sea, bobbing along like so many ducks in the distance. The wind wrapped itself around my ears. The dog began to dig holes and then he chased some gulls.

I was attracted to the idea of numbness and so I took off all my clothes except for my bra and panties and waded in. I pretended that my underwear was in reality a bathing suit. By the time I was knee-deep, I'd lost all feeling in my feet. Doggo had leapt right in with me. He attacked the waves with his teeth. He was fluid and reckless. I dove into the next likely wave to come my way. The shock of cold was so shocking that I staggered to my feet, only to have the next wave knock me down. I took it personally. I decided to swim out into the surf like I meant it. I adopted the "lifeguard" stroke I'd learned one long-ago summer at Bible camp and pointed myself in the direction of Japan.

Eventually I came to a place just beyond the crashing waves where the great sea swells lifted me up and set me down gently. I thought about how those waves had come all this way across the sea to meet me here on the other side. My feet weren't touching. I felt weightless. My good old doggo was running back and forth along the tide line, barking out his frenzied happiness and wagging his tail at me. Now that I had accomplished something extraordinary, I was ready to swim back. That's when I first understood that I'd come here for a purpose far beyond the understandings of my tiny human mind. Something was here with me. Some pagan lord of justice, probably the Crab Queen herself, had led me to recklessly and idiotically swim out to sea in my underwear. I was caught in a fierce strong current, most probably that fabled "riptide" people always talk about. Because it was time for me to pay the piper. Because I was about to die. Because of what I'd done to my Drew, and to Mrs. Brisket, and to Mrs. Brisket's only son. And it was all right with me. I was about to get served my just deserts. All of those people, each one of them, was dead on account of my malicious decision to rip the lips of Mrs. Brisket to begin with. Poor Doggo! He was an innocent bystander, sucked into the vortex of cosmic justice by my perfidy. I told myself someone would surely adopt him. Better for that doggo to be adopted by a good person who happened to be walking along the beach looking for a dog than to stay with a terrible person like me. Let me be sucked out to sea. The sharks would find me soon enough. I accepted it. Just as I was about to go under for good I saw the Crab Queen skimming toward me along the surface of the water to claim me with open arms. I closed my eyes and waited for her claws to snatch me from this life. Only it wasn't the Crab Queen. It was a young surfer. He paddled alongside me casually. He told me to hang on to his board so he could kick-swim me back to the beach. I was too done in to argue with him. I didn't have it in me to explain how necessary it was for me to atone for my sins by drowning. And so I did what he told me to do. The young surfer began to paddle me back to shore. It wasn't as far away as I'd supposed. It wasn't long at all before I had come back to the land of the living.

I lay there, bedraggled, on the damp sand, on my back, breathing in big heaves.

When the young surfer leaned over me to check my vitals, the sun shone behind his head like a magnificent halo.

"Don't worry, Celia. Everything is going to be all right," the young surfer said.

"What?" I said.

"Don't worry, Celia. Everything is going to be all right," he said a second time.

"You can't possibly know that," I said.

He didn't stay to debate me. He was already running back out to sea. When he reached the first line of surf he elegantly flopped on top of his surfboard and paddled away. I watched as he grew smaller and smaller and then he reached the vanishing point and disappeared.

Doggo gamboled up and began to lick my face all over.

There was sand in my teeth, and my ears were ringing.

That night Doggo slept on top of me in the back seat of my

mother's Oldsmobile. He slept badly, though, whining through the night and making sad small sleep-barks in his dreams and at four in the morning he woke me up with small nips. He looked like he'd never felt at home anywhere in this world. I gave him a hug. Then I gave him some water. As he lapped gratefully, I gave myself some life advice. I said to myself: "Celia, you have got to do right by this dog." I couldn't go on sleeping in my car now that I had a dog to take care of. This dog deserved a proper home. He deserved "puppy pads" on the floor of his home, too, until he reliably learned to express his exuberant bowels outdoors. Beyond these considerations, I also knew the dangers posed to canines with owners who unthinkingly left them in cars to suffer heat death and I did not want that to happen to this dog.

I didn't necessarily have a plan as yet about where to go, but a homing instinct had taken over, and as soon as I pulled back onto the road I was compelled to follow that instinct just as migratory birds are compelled to fly north for thousands of miles each spring when they could have just as well stayed in the warm places year-round, and before long I was standing in front of my own house again, with my dear dog standing next to me.

It was early morning, just before dawn, and the dew was rising.

And now I am very tired, my dears, and my mind is cramping. Forgive me if I'm about to skip and gallop and bound ahead and leave whole decades out. I am an old woman. At this age, you never know when your time will come. I need to focus on the most important things in this true-crime story of mine, the things I've still not told you, while I have the energy left in me to tell them.

I won't tell you I came back to life right away because I didn't. To tell the truth, I'd been a little damaged by those wild days I'd lived through, after the death of Vivienne Bianco—days that had led me so explosively and so unexpectedly to a blood-soaked scene of my own making in the living room of the home in which I'd grown up. For years I couldn't think a single thought that didn't include the image of the hole in my husband's former face staring up at me. Eventually I stopped dreaming about him. My posture improved. I gained some weight, almost all of it in my breasts. I filled out, so to speak.

I never went back to work at the phone company. I couldn't tolerate all those voices pouring into my ear. I was too terrified I'd make another blunder and someone else would wind up dead.

I'd had enough of trains, too. I took a job working behind the concessions bar on the Larkspur Ferry. From morning to night I rode back and forth across the bay while serving snacks to commuters. Candy. Chips. Fresh baked goods. I got to know the regulars. Every day I watched the skyline get bigger and bigger as we chugged toward the city, until the buildings loomed high above, and on the way back I'd watch those buildings flow back into the size of a tiny city, set on the other side of the waters. I never grew tired of this spectacle.

On sunny days, the spires of the Golden Gate Bridge reached up toward the brazen California sun, and from the ferry deck I could see all the tiny people, high above, walking back and forth, taking photos of our ferry, and I would think about Mr. Willy, and I would marvel at the distance he had fallen on a day when he'd stepped off that span and changed the course of his life forever.

You will maybe not be so surprised to learn I ended up with Helen. We'd been roommates for years until the day finally came when she told me she loved me, and before long we were grappling. "I feel like I'm swimming!" Helen said. "Holy hell, Celia, it's like I'm swimming in your warm salty sea, and you taste so goddamn good!" And I knew Helen would be taking a dip in my warm salty sea for the rest of her life, and that I would feel the same way about her warm salty sea, and we were together to the very end, by which I mean, until 2020, when a virus came between us.

We were waiting for the ambulance to come.

Our friends kept going to the hospital and not coming back. Those were the times.

Helen was convinced she was about to go on a one-way trip.

"Stop talking like that," I said. "What would I do without you?"

"I know what you'll do," Helen said. "You're going to write

one of those true-crime stories. It's about a girl who wants her husband dead. This girl seems so young and innocent and sweet that you think she'll never do a thing about it, but then things work out so well for her that you have to think maybe this girl is actually a cagey motherfucker."

"Hmm," I said.

"She's what you'd call an evil genius," Helen said.

"Huh," I said. "But you love her, right?"

"Oh yes," Helen said. "That girl is a very sympathetic protagonist. Everyone loves that girl. I love her most of all."

"It's okay, then," I said.

"Of course it's okay," Helen said. "It's why I love her."

"Helen," I said. "I didn't plan it that way. It just happened."

"If you say so," she said.

"If anyone was to blame, it was the Crab Queen," I said.

"Celia, honey, *you* are the Crab Queen," Helen said.

These were the last words my dear heart ever said to me. For as long as we had left together, which was seven minutes, we held on to each other as hard as we could. We weren't wearing masks. There were no masks in those days. Helen rattled and coughed. I cried. Helen had put her anger aside, her former fury at me, for calling that ambulance, for not letting her pass quietly, for holding on to hope, for condemning her to a sterile death, surrounded by strangers—and the ambulance was on its way, and it had come to this, where the only thing we had left between us was to try to memorize every wrinkle, every liver spot, every worry line and smile line before we said good-bye for good.

Two men with bulgy biceps arrived with a stretcher on wheels.

They whisked my dearest love away.

We are never ready for times such as these. Never.

And that's where I've always planned to end it, dears—but wait. In my rush to bring this story to its close, I've skipped recklessly ahead, and something's missing. A beat. A pause. A moment of silence observed between my life with Drew and my life without him. A tipping point. An epiphany. That ineluctable moment when everything changes. First I'll set the scene. Imagine a predawn day. Imagine a girl, nineteen years old and freshly widowed, and with sand in her teeth. Imagine her standing on her own front lawn, with a young doggo by her side—and that girl is me, and I'm looking up at my own house.

The dew is rising.

And you might think I'm about to tell you how good it felt to be home at last. Here I stood, looking up at the windows of the house where I was born—the house where my mother made her lovely tailored clothes while singing Henry Mancini's breakout hit "Moon River" to me in her low clear voice—the house where I'd sat in a big bay window reading the *F* volume of the encyclopedia while stealing glances at that girl across the street, a girl named Joe—the house where I'd once felt safe, and I'd feel that way again, because this was *my* house, my very own house, and there would never again be anyone living inside it who could tell me what was wrong with me, or hold me down for my own good, or strong-arm me, ever again—

And isn't that the way to end it?

But I couldn't make myself go in there.

"Go, go!" I told myself.

I wouldn't listen, even after I reminded myself of all the

things in my house that I loved so much that I could never live without them, like my black knife, and my dirk, and my picture of Dirk, and my late mother's nail file, and those three original Barbie doll heads from days gone by—

And just then I heard a soft gurgly voice whispering close to my ear, and the voice said, "Celia, Celia. Now listen to me. When you were a child, you spake as a child, and thought as a child, but the time has come to put away childish things."

And I knew it was true. I knew right away. I didn't need those things. And I was done with this place. Something new was about to begin, and it was going to begin that same day, just as soon as I got back into my car with Doggo, after which we would drive along meanderingly, looking to the left, and looking to the right, until I found a random pay phone, where I would get out of the car, and call Helen at work, and she would say, "Oh yes, my dear! I've missed you so much! I love dogs!—Come on over!—Come stay!"—

And for years I'd rent my house in Redwood City to Stanford students who didn't mind about the two people who had met their bloody ends in the front room. In fact, they found it exciting.

Later on I'd sell that house to a lovely South Korean family who had come to this land to pursue their Silicon Valley dreams and if they ever found my secret stash of memory-objects—it's possible they did, when they remodeled the house in 1991—then I never heard about it.

But just now I was a nineteen-year-old girl, standing on my skinny front lawn, looking up at my house, with my intrepid dog by my side.

First I said to myself, "This lawn needs mowing badly."

And then I said to myself: "Well, Celia, never mind about the lawn, because it seems you can't make yourself walk into your own house ever again, but maybe you can check what's in your mailbox, at least."

I discovered I could do that. I opened the mailbox. Along with the usual stuff there were seventeen bereavement cards in there. One of those cards was from Augusta. As soon as I saw her childish loopy handwriting on the envelope I felt instantly repentant for the way I hadn't reached out to her after the death of her son. It must have been terrible for my poor grieving mother-in-law. She must have felt so alone. I'd selfishly done my grieving in solitude while driving aimlessly back and forth across this great state and living on potato chips and Jumbo Jacks when I could have been grieving in one place with my mother-in-law. We could have consoled each other.

I opened Augusta's letter.

Celia, I always said you'd be the death of my boy and it has come to pass. I hereby request you release all claim to my son's remains so I can bury him where he belongs, at the right hand of his late father, Alvin Claude Dent, in the historic Alvarado graveyard, where monks and Indigenous peoples are buried side by side, and where it is my dearest wish to one day join them.

Don't come to the service. You will not be welcome.

Yours truly,
Mrs. Alvin Claude Dent

By the time I came to the end of Augusta's letter I was feeling such tender feelings for my poor mother-in-law that I almost wept. Even in her hour of greatest grief Augusta hadn't flipped her lid, the way the last grieving mother I'd crossed paths with had done. Instead of going on a shooting spree, Augusta had tended to practical matters, like funerals, and burials, and I admired her for that. I couldn't blame her for sending a somewhat strident letter to me, either, because I'd been the death of her boy. I decided to say some prayers on her behalf. First I prayed for her happiness. Then I prayed that Augusta would be granted her dearest wish: to be buried in the historic Alvarado graveyard alongside her husband and son and the monks and Indigenous peoples and everyone else who was buried there. Finally I prayed that Augusta would be granted her dearest wish soon, because she deserved it.

Just as I was wrapping up my final prayer for Augusta Dent, the newspaper boy came riding down the middle of the street on his bicycle, throwing a paper on every porch—*thwap! thwap!*—and although the day hadn't yet broken, the sun was just beginning to hum across the far horizons, and the people were coming out of their houses in their robes and slippers to get their papers. When they saw me they froze a little. I wasn't surprised when no one came running over to see how I was doing. I understood their shyness, and forgave them for it. Violent death isn't something you want to chitchat about so early in the morning. When I waved at them they waved back somberly. Some of them nodded to me, to signal that their sympathies were with me. Some of them nodded at Doggo, to signal that they thought he was a very fine dog. They went back inside. The dawn was just about to dawn. I could hear it coming. The hum along the far horizons had become a mighty rumble. Doggo snuffed at my hand. The Pinto was gone, and so was the deer. I'd just then noticed these absences and they delighted me. I thought back on the dream I'd dreamed behind a furniture warehouse in Lancaster. All the particulars were missing, but the mood of the dream still lingered, and a few seconds later when the first blaze of sun blazed over the rooftops, something took hold of me, and for a second or two I understood how happy I was. I stood there breathing. In and out. It was like looking into the sun. It was like looking into the face of God. If I'd tried to hang on to that feeling then I probably would have spontaneously combusted. And so I let the feeling go.

ACKNOWLEDGMENTS

Evil Genius owes its existence to John Cheever. "The Five-Forty-Eight" isn't my favorite Cheever story. That would be "Reunion." But ever since I first read "The Five-Forty-Eight" I've wanted to put a weapon in Ms. Dent's hand, and to give her the confidence to defend herself against Blake's needy fondles.

This novel also owes its existence to my Drew. Drew wasn't his name. I lost track of him decades ago.